ALPHA DRAGON'S TIGER

The Dragonfate Games

HAWKE OAKLEY

/

ONE

Taylor

"EXCUSE ME, young man. Does this fabric make my butt look fat?"

It took me a second to realize the older woman in the aisle was speaking to me. As the stranger's voice pulled me out of focus, I withheld a sigh. I'd been mentally cataloguing patterns and running calculations for my next quilt. Now all the information floated away like dandelion fluff. I'd have to do it all over again later.

"I'm sorry," I said, turning to the woman. "What was that?"

The woman held up a piece of blue cotton fabric against her rump. "I said, does it make my butt look fat? Sexy, even?"

I was not the best judge of what looked sexy on an older woman. Not because I was a gay omega, but because I was single—and had been for a very long time. The data was clear. I was undesirable, and therefore, not well-versed in the sexiness scale.

Still, the lady had asked me a question. Unfortunately, I was the only other person in the aisle, so it would be rude to ignore her.

"Does it make your buttocks look fat?" I repeated bluntly, wondering if she heard how ridiculous it sounded coming out of someone else's mouth.

But she was unflappable. "Yes, dear. That's the question."

"Do you... *want* it to make your buttocks look fat?"

"Yes! Big butts are all the rage, you know. And I must look good for my date next week."

I felt like a deflated balloon. Even large-rumped older women at the quilting store had dates.

Good for her, I thought genuinely.

Other people might have been jealous. But not me. There was no point in being bitter about other people's lives. *Nobody likes a sourpuss*, my alpha father used to say.

Back when I actually spoke to him.

"Dear?"

The woman's voice pulled me out of my thoughts, except it was welcome this time. She watched me expectantly.

"Er, yes, ma'am," I said. "That fabric compliments your... behind quite nicely."

She brightened and laughed. "Oh, aren't you the sweetest! Then two yards of this blue fabric it is. Thank you."

She went to pick up the bolt of fabric, but struggled to carry the huge roll. It was a scene I'd witnessed time and time again at the quilting store—someone small tried to lift a bolt and dropped it, sending yards of fabric spilling all over the floor.

"Here, ma'am." I lifted the bolt easily over my shoulder.

She sighed in relief. "You're my superhero today, aren't you?"

"Not at all."

"Nonsense. Look at those big shoulders and strong muscles! A strong young alpha like you must get plenty of action."

I tried to hold back my wince, but the woman must've noticed. She frowned in concern. "Oh, sorry, dear. Did I say something wrong?"

"No." I placed the bolt on the cutting table. I caught the eye of a nearby employee and waved her over. "There you are, ma'am. Hope that helps."

The older woman opened her mouth to say something but I walked away quickly, hoping she'd get caught up chatting with the employee.

Once I was out of earshot, I was off the hook. I returned to the fabrics I'd been looking at.

Honestly, her assumption didn't upset me that much. At least, I tried to tell myself it didn't. Because of my powerful shoulders and stoic nature, I was frequently mistaken for an alpha. But the real reason my body looked the way it did was because I was a Siberian tiger shifter. Our animal forms were so muscular and strong that even omegas of our kind took on those traits. There was nothing I could do about it.

But I didn't expect a stranger to know that at a glance. It was easier to let people think what they wanted instead of explaining the truth. Especially since, in our society, humans and shifters lived together. Often I didn't know whether the strangers next to me in public were human or not. I'd rather cut off my nose than explain my whole life story to a human: *Yes, I'm an omega, not an alpha. Yes, I know I'm bigger than most omegas you know. Yes, it's because I'm actually a tiger. No, I don't react to catnip...*

That wasn't true. But humans didn't need to know that.

I sighed, pinching the bridge of my broad nose. What was I doing again?

Right. My fabrics. I was in the section of blue cottons, figuring out a pattern for my new quilting project. I'd felt close to a breakthrough when that woman asked for my input, so now I had to think it through all over again.

I ran my hand absentmindedly over the bolts of blue fabric. They were all gorgeous, like the sky or ocean. But they didn't really shine beneath the fluorescent lighting in the shop. I'd need to buy them and take them home to my little sewing room to see their true beauty. It was a cramped room in my small apartment, but it was where the magic happened. And it was *mine*.

"Royal blue next to cobalt blue," I murmured. "Maybe with a baby blue for the binding..."

"Blue this, blue that. How 'bout *red*?"

Another interruption shattered my concentration, but this time it was gratingly familiar. I'd recognize Muzo's voice anywhere.

Before I could turn to look at him, he grunted and dropped a big bolt of red fabric on top of all the blues.

"Geez, that's freakin' heavy!" Muzo grumbled. "How do all the little old ladies shop here?"

I gently pinched his small bicep. "They're all stronger than you, apparently."

"Ouch! Hey, knock it off, I'm not that weak!" Muzo pouted and put his hands on his hips.

Muzo was an omega shifter, too. His animal form was a black-backed jackal, which meant his human form was lithe and wiry—and *much* smaller than me. He looked like a typical omega standing at a cute five-foot-five with narrow hips and a slight frame. But he made up for his size with his obnoxious personality and loud mouth.

"So?" Muzo prompted. "Red? We're going with red, right?"

"*We* are not going with anything. In case you forgot, I'm the one who quilts, not you."

Muzo shrugged. "Meh. How hard could it be?"

"Try it and then we'll talk," I mumbled.

He ignored me and pushed the red bolt of fabric closer to me with an expectant look.

"I'm not using that," I told him bluntly.

"What? Why not? It's a nice fabric. And look, it's red. Don't you *love* red? Doesn't it remind you of the blood of your prey?" Muzo teased.

"Keep your voice down," I growled.

Shifters and humans may have lived together in relative harmony, but that didn't mean it was a utopia. I was conscious of the fact that some humans didn't understand shifters—and when humans didn't understand something, that feeling could easily warp into fear or hatred. Especially of predator species like ours.

"Yeah, yeah," Muzo said, waving me off. "So you don't like it?"

"Red is garish. Put it back."

"Pfft. *Garish*... Such a drama queen."

I stared at him, pointedly raising my eyebrow.

Muzo relented. "Fine, suit yourself. Makin' me carry this heavy thing all the way... Oh gods, my back..."

It was ironic that he called *me* a drama queen when he was the most over-the-top creature I'd ever met in my life. He made a big, pathetic display of trying to pick up the bolt. It was so pathetic that I sighed and took over.

As I hauled the bolt over my shoulder, Muzo grinned. "Aw, thanks, bud! You're a lifesaver. Now if you don't mind, this store is boring me to tears, so I'm gonna check out the cafe next door. Meet me later, okay? See ya!"

I sighed in relief as Muzo darted out the door. Now that he was out of my hair, I could finally look at the damn fabrics in peace. I hadn't even invited Muzo to go shopping with me today. It was like he had a sixth sense for knowing where his friends were so he could annoy them. I wished he had more friends so it wouldn't constantly be *me*.

Just as I put Muzo's displaced red fabric back into its proper place, I heard a yelp and a crash from another aisle.

As a tiger, my reflexes were fast. Within seconds I'd dashed to the source of the sound—my other friend, Poppy, trying not to be crushed by a falling bolt. He shrank to the floor, covering his head with his arms, expecting the weight to drop on him, but I caught it just in time.

"Oh, Taylor, you saved me," Poppy murmured, his big brown eyes wide. He was an Arctic wolf shifter, but his pleading gaze reminded me more of a deer, or a lamb.

I pushed the bolt back to safety. "What were you thinking? This is too high up for you to reach."

Poppy was sensitive, so unlike with Muzo, I spoke to him gently. Even still, Poppy hung his head like I'd admonished him.

"I'm sorry," he said. "I thought you'd like it..."

The fabric that had nearly crushed him into wolf-paste was a deep cerulean blue dotted with yellow stars. It *was* beautiful, and to my taste.

I smiled. "Thanks, Poppy. It's perfect. Just tell me next time. I don't want you to die doing something nice."

He glanced up with a shy smile, looking relieved.

Poppy was an omega, too. Taller than Muzo, shorter than me. But even though he was a wolf shifter, he was unusually delicate. Combined with his soft personality, it made me wonder if he had a difficult past. Even his name was odd. But Poppy never liked talking about himself, and

I never pressured him by asking, so Muzo and I didn't know.

"Why don't you wait with Muzo at the cafe next door? I'll buy my things and we can grab lunch," I suggested.

"Okay."

He seemed pleased that I liked the fabric he chose. As he left, I watched him go to make sure he didn't accidentally get crushed by fabric bolts.

When both my friends had evacuated the fabric shop, I sighed. I couldn't blame them for distracting me. It was my fault for not planning my quilt pattern *before* I arrived.

"I'll figure it out at home," I mumbled to myself.

I gathered the fabrics, had them cut, then paid. I withheld a choking sound when the cashier told me my total.

Quilting was *not* cheap. But it was worth it.

Besides, I had nothing better to spend my human currency on. I was single, had no children, and lived humbly. I had food, a roof over my head, a hobby, and a couple good friends.

My life was fine.

So why did it feel like something was missing?

Holding my purchases, I walked out to the street. My nose wrinkled as traffic drove past. The acrid scent of car exhaust always bothered my sensitive nose. How did humans stand this? Then again, it wasn't like they could shift into a four-legged beast and travel that way. Not that we shifters could, either. Shifting into our animal forms in public was frowned upon, if not forbidden in certain places.

"Hey, Tay!" Muzo called excitedly.

He and Poppy were outside the cafe. There was a small crowd down the street behind them, but I couldn't see what the fuss was about.

Muzo ran towards me. He thrust a small postcard-sized paper into my face. "Look at this!"

I blinked. "What exactly am I looking at?"

"You should enter your name!"

"Muzo, what are you talking about?"

Just as I tried to peek at the card, Muzo snatched it away. "It's a... quilting sweepstakes!"

I perked up. "Quilting sweepstakes? Like a contest?"

Muzo shifted on his feet, still grinning. "Not a contest. More like, you enter your name for a chance to win a huge quilting shopping spree!"

I thought it was odd that the fabric shop wouldn't advertise a sweepstakes *inside* the store, but I had to admit, it piqued my interest.

"Do I have to pay to enter?" I asked suspiciously.

"Nope. Totally free! You know what? Me and Poppy will enter, too. That gives you more chances to win. Obviously, we'd give *you* the prize if we won, our dearest quilter."

"We will?" Poppy asked softly. His brow creased in confusion.

Muzo put his arm around Poppy's shoulder. "Yeah, definitely! I mean, don't we *all* win when our friend does?"

"Um... I suppose," Poppy murmured.

Muzo gasped. "Pops. I am shocked. You *don't* want Taylor to win a fabulous prize?"

Poppy blinked and stammered, "I-I didn't say that!"

"You want him to run out of fabrics. And needles. And yarn."

"Quilting doesn't involve yarn," I grumbled.

Muzo went on, giving Poppy a serious glance. "And whatever else quilters need. Is that what you want, Poppy? You want Taylor to suffer?"

"No!" Poppy cried, as if this was an actual concern.

"Then it's settled. All three of us will enter our names into the quilting sweepstakes." He thrust a fist into the air. "For Taylor!"

People were starting to stare at Muzo's loudmouthed antics.

I sighed. "Okay, don't make a scene about it. Give me the paper."

Muzo thrust it over. The card stock was thick and creamy, the font bold. The text was stark black with gilded borders. Whoever had organized the sweepstakes clearly spared no expense for these entry cards.

Which was odd, because quilting wasn't a particularly flashy hobby.

I looked at the card closer. The bottom and sides were crisp, but the top of the card was feathered, almost like it'd been torn off.

"Mine's like that, too," Muzo said, waving his own identical card. "It must be a design choice. It's thematically appropriate. It marries the robust nature of fabrics with the clean lines in your big patchwork quilts."

I rolled my eyes. Now he was talking out of his ass, as usual. The sooner I put my name on this card and threw it in the running, the better.

"Yours is like that, too, right, Pops?" Muzo asked.

Poppy fiddled with the card in his hand. It too had the same feathered top and crisp edges. "Right..."

Muzo nodded firmly. "See? Design choice."

"Whatever. Give me a pen," I said.

Muzo handed it to me. I scanned the card. The only details it wanted were my name and contact information.

I glanced at Muzo. In the years I'd known him, the sneaky jackal could be... less than truthful. But his white lies never came to any real harm. Even if this entry card was suspicious, I doubted it involved anything dangerous.

My best guess was that Muzo wanted to win a prize and needed two extra entries.

In that case, why didn't he just ask? Dumb dog.

I wrote down my name and information, handed Muzo the entry, then promptly forgot about the probably fictitious sweepstakes.

TWO

Crimson
_____

FOUR MONTHS EARLIER...

"NO."

"But—"

"No," I repeated.

My younger brother Saffron glared at me, his sunshine-yellow eyes narrowing into slits. "Why?"

"Because it's utterly ridiculous. And stop glaring at me. It's not going to accomplish anything. Can you pass me that leg? No, not the half-eaten one."

Saffron huffed as he passed me the raw sheep leg. The smoke that his nostrils exuded charred the meat, giving it a half-cooked scent.

"I didn't ask for it to be medium rare, but thank you," I mumbled.

"And I didn't ask for *you* to shoot down my amazing, world-changing idea without even a second thought," Saffron rebutted. "You're so close-minded sometimes, Crimson. Like a human."

"Please, let's not stoop to that level," I said. "Besides,

this is undoubtedly the worst idea anyone in the history of the planet has ever had."

Saffron bit off a chunk of meat and swallowed. "Do they have theater awards for dragons? If so, you'd win first prize for how dramatic you are."

"Settle down," a deep voice said.

We both looked at our brother, Cobalt. Sheep bones lay beneath his claws. His massive form draped across the mountaintop, his blue scales glinting in the sunlight.

He hadn't said a word since our argument began. Truthfully, I wished he had, so he could be on *my* side. As our eldest brother, he should've been responsible for shutting Saffron down.

"Yes, let's calm ourselves," I said, glancing at Saffron. "No more ridiculous ideas."

Saffron's nostrils flared. Then he drew himself up to engage Cobalt. "Oh, wise older brother of mine, what do you think?"

I rolled my eyes. Sucking up to Cobalt would get him nowhere.

"Please, do tell," I said, looking at him expectantly.

But as Cobalt's silence went on, I worried we weren't on the same page. How could we not be?

"I think," Cobalt said in a deep, slow voice, "that we should bring it up with everybody."

I stared at him. "You are not serious."

Cobalt didn't respond. He tossed a bone into his maw and crunched it into pieces.

Meanwhile, Saffron grinned smugly at me. "See? Cobalt doesn't think it's stupid. And he's way smarter than you, Crimson."

Normally, I'd agree. As our eldest brother, Cobalt was experienced and knew much. But *this*?

I made a face. "If Cobalt says so, then I won't make a fuss."

"Sure..."

I ignored Saffron. Cobalt was only being nice. Otherwise, it made no sense. And Saffron's idea would never get any traction among the rest of us.

Right?

AFTER THE THREE of us returned to the castle, we shifted into our human forms and summoned our family into the dining hall. Gathering seven dragons in one place wasn't an easy task, but Cobalt's roar was a force to be reckoned with. When he got loud, we knew something was up.

Aurum yawned as he sprawled on the table. "Did somebody die?"

Jade pushed up his glasses and gazed around the room with keen emerald eyes. "Clearly not. We're all accounted for."

"Then why'd you wake me up from my nap?" Aurum grumbled.

I leaned back in my chair, crossing my arms. "Because your twin has a grand announcement to make."

Aurum and Saffron were physically identical except for the shade of their hair. Aurum's matched his name, gleaming with a golden hue, while Saffron's hair was the color of sunshine.

Aurum heard the snark in my voice and raised a brow. "Hey, his opinions have nothing to do with me. Unless they're good opinions."

Saffron smirked. "It's good, bro. Trust me."

The two shared an elaborate fist-bump.

I groaned. "The sooner we finish discussing this matter, the better."

Jade heard my disgruntled tone, too. He smirked at me over the horned rims of his glasses. "That bad, is it?"

"Awful," I muttered, ignoring Saffron's glare.

Jade chuckled. "I'm curious to hear what has you in such a sour mood."

"I'm glad my misery entertains you."

Thystle sighed in frustration, cutting us off. "Can we get on with this? Unlike some of you, I'm busy. Not all of us spend all day napping," he snapped, looking at Aurum.

Aurum smiled pleasantly, ignoring the bait. "Yeah, let's get on with it before Thystle has an aneurysm."

Thystle glared like he *was* about to have an aneurysm.

"Cobalt, please," I said. "For the love of Holy Drake, tell us why we're here."

Everyone quieted down. When Cobalt spoke, we listened—unlike with some of our other brothers. With his large form and stoic vibe, he had a powerful presence, like the pull of gravity.

"Earlier today, Saffron proposed a strange idea," Cobalt began.

I sat straighter in my chair, preparing to smirk in Saffron's direction. *Strange* was definitely how I'd describe it.

"But before I relay it, I'd like to remind everyone of one critical fact," Cobalt said. "None of us have mates."

An uncomfortable silence fell across the hall. Saffron and Aurum fidgeted in their seats. Jade sighed. Thystle frowned so hard I was surprised his face didn't fall off. Meanwhile, I rolled my eyes. I already knew what Cobalt was going to say, and it wouldn't help our plight at all.

The only one who didn't react was Viol. Unmoving and unblinking, he watched Cobalt with the same intensity he applied to everything. He was so still that the black-purple iridescent sheen in his hair didn't shimmer as it usually did.

Viol was my beloved brother, but gods, he was unnerving.

"This can't go on," Cobalt said. "It's bad enough that humans don't believe in dragons, but now shifters are losing faith in us."

Aurum snorted, kicking his boots up on the table. "Who cares? They're just jealous *they* aren't dragons."

For once, I was inclined to side with him. Dragons were a special breed, after all.

"Are you stupid or something?" Thystle shot at him. "We're literally related to all shifters, dragon or not. Don't shit-talk them."

Aurum smiled fake-sweetly at him. "How are you the most inclusive dragon in the world, and yet still the biggest asshole?"

The gold dragons and Thystle glared at each other.

"Thystle is correct," Jade pointed out calmly. "As you know, we share a common ancestor—Holy Drake. That is why dragons can breed with all shifters, regardless of species."

Thystle looked smug. "Told you."

"Okay, yeah, fine," Aurum said, waving him off. "But I'd rather mate with another dragon. Wouldn't you?"

"No, because I'm not a speciesist."

Aurum groaned, slumping into his seat. "Here we go... Wake me up when Thystle's done with his lecture."

Elbowing his twin in the side, Saffron asked, "Can you at least listen to my idea before deciding Thystle's an annoying asshole?"

"I can literally hear everything you're saying," Thystle said in an irritable deadpan.

I rubbed my temples. I could only take so much of the younger half of my brothers before a headache assaulted me.

As if sensing my mental anguish, Jade chimed in. "Regardless of your preferences, Aurum, it's a biological fact that dragon shifters can breed with any shifter. It's an unfortunate reality that not many dragons are left. So unless you'd like to mate with one of us—which is possible but biologically useless, since we're all alphas—your choices are limited."

Aurum wrinkled his nose. "Oh, good. My choices are brother-ass or generic wolf-ass."

"Brother-ass is a genetic dead end, I'm afraid," Jade said with a smile.

I withheld a snort of laughter.

"Cobalt." Viol's deep, dangerous voice cut through the amusing atmosphere like a knife. "Speak."

The rest of us piped down. Nobody wanted to incur Viol's wrath. His tone implied that he had places to be, shit to do—likely involving violence—and he wanted to get the fuck out of this family meeting ASAP.

I was also ready to end this silly conversation, but for different reasons. I had a hoard of suits to attend to.

"We need mates," Cobalt announced. Nobody disputed this fact. "We need a catalyst. An event. Instead of wasting our time scouring the land, we need to bring the mates to us."

Saffron perked up, grinning with enthusiasm. At the same time, I felt my hopes crash to the floor. Cobalt wasn't *seriously* considering Saffron's idea... was he?

Cobalt went on. "Saffron suggested hosting a game show to invite omegas to our island and compete for our love, and the right to breed with us."

There it was. Finally, the idiotic suggestion was out in

the open for everyone to hear. I scanned the table eagerly, waiting to hear everyone's raucous laughter.

Except there was none.

"Guys?" I said when nobody spoke.

Jade rubbed his chin thoughtfully. "I see. That's a convenient idea. Not only does it increase the possible options by making multiple omegas compete, but it brings them straight to us."

My jaw dropped.

"Game show!" Aurum cried, high-fiving Saffron. "Dude, that's awesome!"

Saffron grinned back. "I told you!"

Across from them, Thystle huffed. "A game show, huh? That's so dumb it might actually work."

My hopes crashed faster than a city collapsing under dragonfire.

"You all cannot be serious," I muttered.

Saffron stuck his tongue out at me in a childish I-told-you-so gesture. "Get over it, Crimson. Everybody likes my idea except you."

I turned desperately to Viol, who hadn't said a word since ordering Cobalt to speak. But even my crazy brother didn't seem to agree with me. A tiny smirk appeared on the edge of his lips and he gave a slight nod.

That was the final nail in the coffin. I was sorely outnumbered. Arguing with six brick walls would've been a better use of my time.

Yet I still couldn't let it go. Somebody had to be the voice of reason. Usually it was Jade, but he'd betrayed me by laying the positives on the table. Useless green lizard.

"Is anybody thinking about the logistics of this?" I argued. "For one thing, it sounds expensive."

"We have the money," Cobalt pointed out.

"Yes, but *how* are we going to host a game show?

Where will these omegas stay? Who's going to feed them? What if they make a mess of the island? What if—"

Aurum cut me off. "What if Crimson stopped throwing a temper tantrum like a dragonet?"

"I am a grown dragon, thank you very much," I snapped. "One who thinks the idea of finding your mate on a *game show* is vulgar and lowbrow."

The golden twin waved me off. "Yeah, yeah. Keep complaining when we're surrounded by cute omegas, getting laid."

By now I was fuming. "I do not want to *get laid*. I want my fated mate, the love of my life. And he's certainly not going to appear on a Drake-damned game show."

Saffron smiled cloyingly. "Aww, it's actually kinda cute how much of a romantic you are, Crimson."

"Yeah, relax, man," Aurum said, patting me on the arm. "We wanna find our mates as much as you."

I doubted that. Aurum and Saffron were too busy goofing around to think about mates. Me, on the other paw? It crossed my mind multiple times a day. It was an itch I couldn't scratch, and with the length of my talons, it should've been possible to scratch anything.

But then again, this *was* Saffron's idea. Perhaps I'd misjudged my brothers' intentions. Maybe on the inside, they were as lonely as me. That thought filled me with a scrap of sympathy, and guilt for insisting Saffron's suggestion was utter stupidity. Even though it was.

I sighed and pinched the bridge of my nose. "Okay. Who's going to plan and do all the paperwork and red-tape nonsense? Because I won't be roped into it."

Jade snaked his arm around my shoulder with a calming smile. "Relax, Crimson. I don't mind doing it."

Aurum snorted. "Yeah, don't you know paperwork is Jade's kink?"

Jade played along with a good-natured grin. "Oh, absolutely. I'm getting all hot and bothered just thinking about it."

I removed Jade's hand from my arm. "Great. Maybe you can go be horny about paperwork over *there* and not right next to me."

Aurum, Jade and Saffron snickered.

As Cobalt stood from the table, we turned to look at him. He announced, "It's settled. We'll put Saffron's idea into motion. Prepare yourselves. Soon our island will be home to many omegas, all vying for our attention. If it goes well, we might even get a few eggs out of it."

A few of my brothers looked excited at the idea. I withheld the urge to gag.

"You're all missing something important," Thystle said with a disgruntled huff. "This... *thing*—"

"Game show," Saffron supplied.

"This game show needs a name. Something catchy. Otherwise, people won't be interested." Thystle crossed his arms. "This *is* gonna be televised, right?"

Dear Holy Drake. I hadn't even considered that.

"Oh, good," I mumbled. "Not only are we hosting an omega mating party on our home turf, we're actively broadcasting it for the world to see."

Everyone ignored me.

"Yes. It should be televised," Cobalt said confidently. "Dragons have been fading from the public consciousness for a long time now. The more eyes we get on us, the better."

In a supremely unhelpful manner, Jade chimed in, "Game shows run in multiple seasons, correct? It stands to reason that we should follow that formula."

Saffron gasped, leaping up eagerly. "Yeah! Like one of

us per season! That way, we can really focus on the omegas."

"And *they* can focus on *us*," Aurum said, grinning.

The atmosphere in the hall buzzed. Everybody was enthusiastic about this—except me. True love couldn't blossom on reality TV. A thousand pitfalls of this concept ran through my head: omegas coming on the show for fame, omegas wanting a paid vacation, omegas who'd only pretend to fall in love with us for our money...

Why didn't my brothers understand?

It was useless voicing my concerns. They were all smitten with the idea.

I was too busy sulking to tune into the conversation until Aurum mentioned my name.

"...think Crimson should go first."

"Excuse me?" I asked.

Everybody turned to look at me.

I blinked, narrowing my eyes. "What?"

Cobalt spoke up. "Aurum said you should go first."

"What, on a slide? In a conga line?"

I saw Aurum gearing up to insult me before Cobalt stepped forward. I wasn't short by any means, but my older brother towered over me, his imposing presence commanding my attention.

"You should be the star of the first season," Cobalt said.

"The star," I echoed. As his meaning slowly sank in, my eyes widened in horror. "You mean... you want *me* to be the face of season one of this vulgar game show?"

"Yes."

They were fucking with me. They were all fucking with me. This had to be some kind of elaborate plot to cause me to have a mental breakdown, because I was on my way to one.

But Cobalt's expression was serious. As usual.

I felt like a worm on a fishhook, writhing violently for survival to no avail. It was too late. My brothers had already decided my fate for me.

Assholes.

"Are you sure I won't tank your ratings with my sour attitude?" I asked snidely.

Aurum grinned. "No way. People *love* sassy, handsome men like you. You'll probably go viral."

As I mulled over that backhanded compliment, Cobalt nodded.

"We'll work out the logistics," he promised. "All you need to do is show up."

I wrinkled my nose but didn't argue. If that was all, then it didn't sound too awful. It wasn't like I'd *actually* fall in love with any of the omega contestants. Fake reality TV romance happened all the time. As long as I created good TV, the show would go on. Then my brothers who truly wanted to be on this game show could have their turn.

I sighed loudly. "Fine."

The golden twins grinned in satisfaction. Thystle pretended to examine his nails, but was clearly enthused. Jade smiled calmly, and Cobalt seemed satisfied, despite his stoic face.

Viol suddenly stood from his seat, causing it to scrape against the hardwood floor.

"The Dragonfate Games," Viol growled. "That's what we'll call it."

Without another word, he stalked outside, shifted into dragon form behind the windows, and flew off.

Jade smiled mildly at the rest of us. "Well, I suppose there's no arguing with that."

"The Dragonfate Games, huh?" Aurum beamed. "That's actually perfect!"

I had to admit, it was better than my idea, *The Stupid Waste of Time Games*.

Saffron lapsed into a catchy sing-song tune. "The Dragonfate Games, gonna learn our fated mates' names!"

Thystle groaned. "Now that's gonna be stuck in my head for a week..."

I shook my head, sharing Thystle's misery. The earworm was wedged in my brain, too.

"Well," I announced, "if nobody needs me urgently, I'm going to go mope."

"Go ahead and enjoy your moping session," Jade urged with an amused look. "We'll find you when we need you."

I followed in Viol's footsteps. Outside the castle, I shifted into my dragon form and launched into the sky. The cold wind whipping against my scales cooled off my temper, but it couldn't stop the mix of looming anxiety and disdain from roiling in my stomach.

The Dragonfate Games... What a joke. No matter what happened, I vowed never to find my mate in such a ridiculous fashion.

THREE

Taylor

A BLARING, raucous sound woke me at 8AM sharp.

I never slept in so late, but last night's sleep had been plagued by uncomfortable dreams. I'd tossed and turned until the small hours of the morning. My eyes felt sticky and tired when the phone blasted me awake.

Grumbling, I snatched the accursed thing off my nightstand. I must've forgotten to put it on do-not-disturb like I usually did.

I checked the screen. Instead of a number, the caller ID said "CHROMATIMAEUS OFFICE."

I blinked, squinting at the odd name. At first I thought I'd misread it, since I was still battling consciousness, but I'd read it correctly. What kind of office name was that?

But an office was an office. Besides the weird name, the ID didn't look shady. I picked up the call.

"Hello?" I said gruffly.

A peppy feminine voice replied, "Hi there! This is Winnie from the Chromatimaeus Island office. Am I speaking with Taylor Chalchin?"

Those words made my brain feel like soup. I sat up, rubbing my eyes. "Yes, this is him."

"Let me be the first to say congratulations!" Winnie exclaimed.

Now I was really confused. "Um... for what exactly?"

"Taylor, your application was approved! You've been selected to participate in the Dragonfate Games!"

Was I still dreaming? I didn't know what the hell this woman was talking about, or why she sounded so peppy about it.

"I'm sorry, I have no idea what's going on," I admitted.

Winnie paused for a second, then continued in an upbeat voice. "Oh! Um, do you remember submitting an application to appear on a TV program?"

I couldn't help the derisive snort that came out of me. "Sorry, no. I'd never do anything like that. I think you have the wrong number."

A keyboard clacked on the other end of the line. "Taylor Chalchin, omega Siberian tiger shifter, age twenty-seven. Is that correct?"

I paused, frowning. All of that information was true.

"How do you know all that?" I asked.

Winnie sounded baffled, but kept her professional customer service voice equipped. "You provided it." She paused. "Well, except your age. We found that out from a quick background search."

I bolted upright and paced my bedroom. "Okay, wait. Just... hang on. Why are you performing background searches on me? What is this call even about?"

Sensing my confused frustration, Winnie explained in a gentle, friendly voice. "So, a few weeks ago, you submitted your name and contact info for an opportunity to enter the Dragonfate Games, a televised dating experience."

My brain felt scrambled. Dragonfate Games? Televised dating experience?

I rubbed my temples. How could I tell this woman I

wasn't interested in whatever she was selling without sounding like a dickhead?

"I don't want to be on some reality TV show," I said in a strained voice. "I don't even *own* a TV. And I never submitted my name and contact—"

I froze.

That wasn't true. I *had* submitted my name and contact info to enter *something*. Except I'd been tricked into thinking it was a quilting sweepstakes, not a gods-damned reality dating show.

I ground my teeth and hissed. "*Muzo.*"

"Sorry?" Winnie asked.

I couldn't vent at this poor woman who was just doing her job. I huffed. "Look, this has all been a big misunderstanding. My idiotic friend told me I was entering a quilting contest, not... whatever this is."

Winnie's nails clacked against the keyboard. "What's the name of this idiotic friend?"

"Muzo."

"Is that a Muzo Zavala?"

I frowned deeper. "Yes. How'd you know?"

"He's also been accepted to enter the Dragonfate Games! That means the two of you will share food, lodging, the whole experience. Only one contestant can win, so for the one who goes home, it's basically an extended paid vacation. We also deal with contacting your workplaces to assure time off, and set up transportation services—all complimentary, of course."

My head spun. None of what she said felt real.

"Is this a scam?" I asked bluntly.

Winnie laughed. "No, but I can see why you'd think that, Mr. Chalchin! It's not often this kind of opportunity happens to people."

I sat back down on my bed, feeling winded. "Do you, like, want money from me?"

She laughed casually. "Nope. Like I said, we pay for the whole experience. All you have to do is show up—and maybe fall in love."

I ignored the second half of her sentence. "Who is *we?*"

"The dragon brothers of Chromatimaeus Island. I'm just their secretary. They're the ones who organized this event."

That hit me like a freight train. I nearly dropped my phone.

"Dragon brothers...?" I murmured. "But dragons aren't real."

There was a hint of sympathy in Winnie's voice as she chuckled. "They're super real, Mr. Chalchin. They pay my bills." She giggled. "If you accept the offer, you'll meet them in the flesh."

I couldn't believe it.

Dragons.

Dragons were real—and they organized a fucking reality TV dating show?

I fought the urge to tell Winnie that this all sounded like a load of crap. As much as I didn't want to believe her, I did. It was too ridiculous to be a lie.

"So what am I supposed to do?" I asked. "Just drop my whole life to go on some reality TV show where a rare, handsome dragon could possibly choose me to be his mate?"

Apparently, Winnie did not pick up on my sarcasm, because she chipperly replied, "Yep, that's right!"

I sighed. What a hassle.

"I sense your hesitation, so let me try to persuade you," she said in a friendly manner. "It's an all-expenses-paid experience. You won't have to spend a single dime. We take care of travel, lodging, food, everything you can imagine."

"Right, because they're rich dragons, right?"

Once again, my snarky comment flew over her head. Either that, or she was pointedly ignoring it, in which case, well played.

"Yep!"

"What about my job?" I asked. "Not everybody can afford to just drop their work and prance off to some fancy island."

I did actually have a reserve of vacation time, but I didn't tell that to her. At this point, I just found myself playing devil's advocate, trying to think of some reason why I shouldn't do this.

She chuckled. "We take care of that. The brothers want this to be a stress-free experience for all the omegas involved."

My eyes twitched. That was right. If I accepted, I wouldn't be the only omega on the island. There'd be tons of them running around and vying for a dragon's attention. I rolled my eyes. How pathetic could you get?

And yet, despite my distaste for the idea, I was strangely intrigued. Dammit.

I suddenly remembered something. Muzo and I weren't the only ones who'd entered the supposed quilting sweepstakes.

"Winnie, can I ask if there is another contestant I know?"

She hummed. "Well, I'm not technically supposed to give out that information, but for you, I'll make an exception." I could practically hear her winking.

"Thanks. Is there a Poppy Faolan on the list?"

Keys clacked. "There most certainly is!"

I felt relieved. Poppy was sensitive. It would've hurt his feelings if the two of us were accepted and he wasn't. More than anything, he hated being alone.

I pinched the bridge of my nose and exhaled slowly. What would happen if I didn't accept this offer? I thought of my friends on this remote dragon island. Would Muzo get into trouble? Would Poppy get bullied by the other contestants? Was it safe to just let them go?

I grumbled, pacing more. It wasn't like I was their parent or anything, but I couldn't help feeling protective of my friends. They needed me to watch over them.

Or… that was just the excuse I needed to go.

Winnie waited patiently on the other end of the line. I found that comforting. If this had been some elaborate scam, she would've rushed me into accepting.

"I don't know," I mumbled. "This is all so much, so fast."

"I understand. If you like, I can give you a day or two to think about it. But if you don't have an answer by then, I'll be forced to move on to the waitlist."

"Why me?" I asked. Out of all the people who'd entered for a chance to date a dragon, why was my name chosen?

"All the names were randomly selected," Winnie explained. "So who knows? Maybe it's fate, after all."

A shiver went down my spine.

Fate. That was laughable. As if anyone would ever find their fated mate on a stupid reality TV show.

It was almost so stupid that I didn't want to pass up the opportunity.

There was a long pause before Winnie said, "Well, Mr. Chalchin—"

"Taylor. And…" I blew out a long breath. "Fine. I accept the offer."

Winnie audibly brightened. "Yay! I'll email you the contract and all the other information you need. You won't regret this, Taylor."

I didn't know why, but I was inclined to agree.

FOUR

Crimson
―――――――――

TODAY WE WERE SHOOTING a commercial for the Dragonfate Games. I couldn't think of anything I'd rather do less, but at least I got to riffle through my hoard and pick out a nice suit to show off to the world.

I strolled through the custom walk-in closet in my bedroom. Hundreds of quality suits hung on the racks surrounding me. My hand grazed over their fine fabrics as I walked by, the sensation of it calming me. If I closed my eyes and breathed deeply, I could smell the delicate aroma of the Merino wool.

This was my happy place. I could've sat in the middle of my hoard all day. Unfortunately, I'd been roped into this mind-boggling TV show and it was too late to escape.

"Let's see," I murmured to myself. I scanned the line of suits, wondering which one I wanted to feature. It was impossible to choose—they were all so beautiful.

"I wish those lizard brains chose a fashion show instead of a dating one," I grumbled.

"Still moping?"

Jade strolled in with a wry smile. Although the aisle was spacious, he was still careful not to brush against any of my suits. Despite the fact that we were brothers, it was considered deeply rude to touch another dragon's hoard without permission. I was even more anal about it than most dragons—just seeing Jade standing inside my closet made my skin itchy.

Fortunately, he was one of my more conscientious siblings. He must've seen the annoyance on my face and stepped back out of the closet.

"Sorry," Jade said. "They sent me to fetch you since you were taking so long."

I made a sour face. "I can't help it. How am I supposed to choose a suit? Look at them. They're all works of art."

Jade didn't comment on the peculiarity of my hoard. Every dragon's hoard was unique.

"Would it help if I picked one for you?" Jade suggested.

I squinted. "You're not going to touch it, are you?"

"No, grumpy pants. I'll point at it."

The childish name didn't sound so bad coming from him. On the other hand, if the golden twins had said it, I'd want to wring their little necks.

"Fine," I relented.

"Close your eyes. I'll surprise you."

I rolled my eyes for good measure before shutting them. "Like you're going to surprise me with a mate?"

"You know, if you really don't want to do it, just say so," Jade said patiently. "You're a big, bad fire-breathing dragon. We can't force you to do anything."

"So are the rest of you," I reminded him.

"You're right. We should all threaten to incinerate you if you don't comply."

"Are you making fun of me?"

Jade sounded amused. "No. I'd never do such a thing."

I huffed. Jade was so calm and down to earth that it was impossible to get annoyed at him. Admittedly, his presence was soothing. I was glad he showed up to help, otherwise I would've been trapped by indecision in this closet forever.

"And... this one," Jade said.

I opened my eyes. He pointed at a gorgeous chocolate-brown suit. The smooth, rich color was unconventional, but striking.

Jade nodded at my head. "It looks good with your human hair," he explained. "And the unusual colour will help viewers remember you."

"I don't need viewers to remember me," I said half-heartedly.

"You're right. The whole point of this is to find a mate, not become a TV icon." Jade smiled. "But reminding people—shifters and humans—that dragons exist is a good thing."

I grimaced but didn't argue with him. As we faded from public consciousness, our magic grew weaker. We were still highly powerful magical beings, of course, but we didn't strike fear and awe in people like we once did. Now we were too often relegated to fairy tales or myths.

A sudden uneasiness hit me. What if nobody applied to be on the show because they didn't believe dragons were real?

I shook the thought from my head. What foolishness. As if I actually cared about this Dragonfate Games nonsense...

I took the rich brown suit carefully from the rack and examined it in front of the full-length mirror. My reflection was crystal-clear, since our housekeeper shined the mirror to perfection.

"It looks great on you," Jade commented.

He was right. The smooth color of the suit worked well with the natural red streak in my otherwise black hair. I'd be offended if the omegas *didn't* find me attractive.

Not that I cared. Because I wasn't going to pick any of them to be my mate. This was all for my brothers' sakes. Nothing more.

After getting dressed, Jade took me to the pier by the beach. My stomach twisted when I saw the film crew already set up. My brothers—except Viol—were all present. Judging by their impatient faces, I'd kept them waiting.

"Finally," Aurum said with a groan. "What took you so long? All this equipment is melting under the sun."

"Be nice to your older brother," Jade chided him gently. "It's tough to be the first dragon ever on TV. Right, Crimson?"

"I suppose," I mumbled.

The director clapped his hands. "Places, everyone. Let's get ready to shoot this commercial."

Everybody rushed around. My brothers and the staff all had tasks. Meanwhile, I stood there like a dressed-up doll with nothing to do.

I glanced over at a nearby table with papers on it. It seemed to be information about the show.

As the sea breeze fluttered, the papers rustled. Something caught my eye. There were multiple photographs of human faces.

No, not humans. Shifters.

They were the first contestants of the Dragonfate Games.

Curious, I edged closer to the table. The photographs were half-hidden beneath a paperweight.

I got the feeling I wasn't supposed to be looking at them. But seeing as I had no intention of actually falling in love with any of the contestants, did it really matter?

Still, it felt a bit naughty to be looking at them. I glanced up to where the staff and my brothers ran around dealing with the commercial. None of them paid me any attention.

What was a bored dragon to do?

I nudged the paperweight aside. Now I could get a good look at all the photos. I idly flipped through them like magazines in a waiting room. Every photo was accompanied by a description of the omega's name and shifter species. None of them caught my eye, obviously. They were all decently attractive men, sure, but it was laughable to think I'd ever fall in love with any of them. A man who'd participate in a reality TV dating show like this was *so* not my type.

Yawning, I flipped through to the last page.

I froze.

At the very bottom of the page was the last contestant. His photo made my heart skip a beat.

And that *never* happened to me.

But a dragon's curiosity couldn't be contained. We were like giant, scaly cats.

Instead of walking away, I examined the photo. The omega had well-combed, dusky blond hair, dark almond-shaped eyes, a strong nose, and a handsome jaw.

But it was his stoic expression that seized me. Unlike the other contestants, he wasn't smiling, yet he didn't look unfriendly. It was like he was looking directly into my soul.

Impossible. It was just a damn photo.

I scanned his description.

Taylor Chalchin. Age 27. 5'10". Siberian tiger shifter.

On their own, none of those traits meant anything. But all together, and combined with his striking photo, they did something to me. I wanted to know more about him on an instinctual level. What was he like? How was his personality? Was he as handsome in person as he was in his photo?

I snorted. None of that mattered. Just like the rest of the applicants, Taylor wasn't my type. He *couldn't* be. As if I'd ever be fated to an omega who voluntarily participated in a reality TV dating show…

Then again, I'd been swept up in the chaos of it against my will. Maybe Taylor had six annoying brothers who'd forced him into this, too…

Without noticing, my hand had moved across the paper. My fingers brushed against Taylor's portrait.

Sucking in a sharp breath, I yanked my hand away. Why was I tenderly caressing a fucking piece of paper?

The rapid motion drew Thystle's attention. Frowning —as usual—he stormed over and snatched my wrist, pulling me towards the filming zone.

"What the hell are you doing? You're not supposed to look at those," he snapped.

"There wasn't much to see," I replied in a snarky tone.

But that wasn't entirely true. My mind drifted back to Taylor, remembering how his feline gaze had struck me.

Thystle huffed. "Well, whatever. I know you're gonna brood and sulk the whole time, so I guess it doesn't matter that you got a sneak peek of the contestants."

"You're one to talk about brooding and sulking," I teased.

He glared before throwing me toward the stage. The camera crew gestured for me to smile, pointed at the prompter, then began filming.

The whole time, all I could think about was that stoic tiger ferociously staring back at me.

FIVE

Taylor

"HOLY CRAP!" Muzo exclaimed. "Look at the size of that landing strip!"

That earned us a bunch of awkward stares from the other local contestants waiting to board. I ground my teeth, pulling Muzo into a gentle yet restraining headlock.

"Can you please refrain from yelling and causing a scene?" I muttered. "Especially when it involves innuendos?"

"Who's making innuendos? Get your mind out of the gutter. I'm clearly talking about the literal landing strip." He grinned and wiggled his eyebrows, obviously not as innocent as he claimed to be.

The waiting area was spacious. I appreciated the ability to keep away from the other contestants. Not because I was unfriendly, but because *they* all teemed with excitement about the Dragonfate Games. I couldn't go a minute without hearing someone gush about dragons, or being on TV, or gloating about the amazing selfies they were taking.

It got old fast.

Still, I made a conscious effort not to be too cranky

about it. After all, these people were omega shifters, just like me. It wasn't often I was in a place without humans.

All of the accepted participants in our area had been asked to arrive at this private airport. Looking around, I didn't see more than two dozen men. Would more of them arrive at the island from different locations?

"I've never been on a plane before," Poppy murmured. He sank back in his seat and glanced anxiously at the huge bay window where the plane awaited us. "Are they scary?"

Muzo draped over the back of his seat. "Pops, everything is scary to you."

If I was in tiger form, I would've cuffed him over the head with my paw. I settled for a verbal warning. "Knock it off, Muzo. He has a point. Wolves aren't supposed to be in the air."

"Neither are tigers or jackals," Muzo pointed out, then yawned. "Are we gonna board or what? We've been here for an hour. I'm gonna go ask the people at the desk."

I sighed as he scampered off. Hanging out with him was like babysitting a hyperactive child sometimes.

"Don't worry, it's safe," I said to Poppy. "I'll sit right next to you, okay?"

He nodded, looking relieved. He'd bought a paperback novel from one of the airport shops to distract himself, but instead of reading it, he fiddled with the pages.

"I can't believe Muzo tricked us like that," Poppy said.

"I can," I mumbled. "The part I can't believe is that we both accepted the offer."

Poppy smiled slightly. "No one's ever picked me for anything. When they called me, I thought it was one of those scams you're always warning me about…"

I snorted. "I did, too. No opportunity could be this perfect. But I guess being rich has some benefits."

Poppy shuffled his feet. "Do you really think we're going to meet dragons?"

"I would hope so," I said dryly. "It *is* called the Dragon-fate Games. Besides, I imagine only dragons would spend big money on something as stupid as this."

Behind me, somebody sniffed loudly. We turned around to see a young white-haired omega with crossed arms.

"Do you think talking badly about your benefactors is appropriate?" he asked, raising a penciled-on brow.

I didn't know who this guy was, or why he bothered sucking up to people who weren't even here, but I wasn't about to let some little punk come at me with that attitude.

"Oh, I'm sorry," I said sarcastically. "I didn't know my conversation was an open forum."

The omega sneered. He had a fake, powdery smell that smothered his natural scent, so I couldn't tell what type of shifter he was.

"Sounds like something a first-out would say," he said with a haughty tone, as if he'd just let loose an epic burn.

Sensing Poppy's distress, I turned back around without giving the random omega another second of my time. He was the type of person who got upset from being ignored. I sensed him fuming behind me.

"Looks like they're ready to board," I said to Poppy. "Want to head over there together? I'll get your luggage."

Poppy nodded, eager to be away from the confrontation. I knew he was sensitive about that sort of thing. Grabbing the handles of both our suitcases, I dragged them towards the boarding area.

To nobody's surprise, Muzo was at the head of the line. He grinned and waved us over, earning him grumpy looks from the people between us. I shook my head. When we didn't join him, Muzo frowned, sighed, and dragged his luggage towards us.

"C'mon, I wanted to sit together," he whined.

"This isn't a field trip, you know," I reminded him. "Besides, it's a big plane. There's plenty of space for us to sit together. Not that I necessarily want to."

He let out a *snrk* of laughter and elbowed me playfully. "You know you love me."

"Some days it's debatable."

As the three of us waited in line, I heard a familiar haughty voice behind us say, "Oh, good. You're multiplying."

Not that white-haired omega again. I rolled my eyes and mouthed, "don't give him any attention," but it was already too late. In any situation, Muzo jumped in first and asked questions later.

"Who the hell are you?" Muzo said, raising a brow.

I cursed Muzo for asking. This was the opportunity that haughty asshole had been waiting for. I could practically feel the raw smugness oozing out of the omega's body.

"My name is Alaric. You'd do well to remember it, since I'll be the undisputed winner of the Dragonfate Games."

Muzo casually sniffed the air. "Why do you smell like a baby's ass?"

Never mind. I take back everything I said about Muzo. Hearing Alaric's mortally offended gasp was worth it.

"It's *perfume*," Alaric shot back. "Very expensive, and clearly not a brand you recognize. And it does *not* smell like a baby's bottom."

"Ass," Muzo said.

From the corner of my eye, I saw Alaric's white arm hair standing on end with fury. It reminded me of an animal's hackles rising. I figured he was some kind of mammal shifter, at least. Even while standing next to him, it was impossible to tell. He really *did* smell like a baby's freshly powdered ass.

Poppy tugged on my sleeve. "Um, the line's moving."

I nodded. "Thanks, Poppy. Let's get on the plane."

Muzo wriggled his fingers at Poppy. "It's about to gobble us up! We're gonna sit in its big plane tummy!"

"Are you eight years old?" I grumbled. "Leave Poppy alone."

Behind us, Alaric sniffed loudly. "I thought you had to be at least 18 to apply."

"I don't remember inviting you to this conversation," I said without looking at him.

Sensing Poppy's anxiety, I put my hand on his shoulder as the lady at the counter took our tickets with a big smile and told us to have a great flight. I wondered if she was human, or some kind of shifter hired by the bigwig dragons.

"Tunnel!" Muzo yelled as we entered the tunnel connecting the airport with the plane.

I sighed and didn't bother telling him to behave. He was like a kid who'd eaten three pounds of sugar. What would happen when filming began? Would Muzo even last one day, or would the dragons send him packing?

I thought of Poppy, too. He shuffled beside me, clutching his backpack tightly to his chest. I was honestly surprised he'd accepted the offer to join the Games.

"Hey, Poppy," I said quietly as we waited for the people in front of us to enter the plane. "Why did you decide to join, anyway?"

"Um... I don't know." Poppy put a hand to his shirt. "I got this weird feeling in my chest."

"Anxiety?" I suggested.

"No. Well... yes, but something else, too. An important feeling. I knew I had to try, even though I was scared."

I smiled. "I'm proud of you. It's not easy to push past your fear."

Poppy smiled back. "Thanks, Taylor."

"Oh, so the big brute has a name," Alaric remarked.

My annoyance sizzled into anger. Alaric had yanked on the tiger's tail too much.

I whirled on him with a snarl. I felt my canine teeth elongating into thick fangs. It was something I held back when I was among humans, but everyone was a shifter here, so I didn't feel pressured to contain the beast.

"Listen," I growled. "Stop butting your head into my life. Mind your own business, and I'll mind mine."

Alaric's eyes flashed, but he didn't move. I noticed for the first time that he had heterochromia—one eye was blue, the other green.

"Touchy, touchy," Alaric mumbled. "You think you can boss people around with your *bulk*? Well, I won't stand for it. The winner of the Dragonfate Games will have poise. They won't need to bully their way to victory."

"Who's bullying anyone?" I demanded, annoyed and baffled.

Alaric smirked. He glanced at the other contestants watching us. I noticed how the scene must've looked—a broad-shouldered, tall man snarling at a shorter, slimmer one. Alaric had tricked me into looking like a villain.

With a flash of shame and irritation, I reined in my tiger. Normally I had better control of myself. The stress of this TV show was getting to me and it hadn't even started yet.

Poppy grabbed my arm and led me. Usually I was the one who comforted him, but now he returned the favor. I felt myself relax.

A smiling middle-aged man who I assumed to be the pilot welcomed us on board. "Have a great flight! We're just finishing up the magic fueling, then we'll be on our way."

"Magic fueling?" Muzo asked, brows shooting up to his hairline.

The pilot nodded. "That's right. Our team of wyvern engineers fuel the plane with magic. One of the dragon brothers in charge, Cobalt, was insistent the Games be as environmentally friendly as possible."

That was a pleasant surprise compared to all the human superstars with no qualms about polluting the air for the sake of their personal convenience.

"Whoa!" Muzo cried. "Did you hear that, Taylor? Not just dragons, but wyverns, too! And magic! This is not a drill—this is really happening, people!"

Alaric cleared his throat and addressed the pilot. "Is Cobalt the dragon whose affections we will compete for?"

The pilot gave a mellow laugh. "Well, I'm probably not supposed to tell you... but no, it's not Cobalt. Different color."

Poppy blinked. "Cobalt...?"

"He said different color, Pops," Muzo said. "Think green, or yellow, or whatever. Anyway, let's board already, I'm tired of waiting around!"

As a group of three, we found our seats. The inside of the plane was surprisingly spacious and comfortable. Muzo took the window seat, Poppy sat securely in the middle, and I took the aisle, since I didn't care where I sat.

Alaric shot me the stink eye as he passed, but we kept our jabs to ourselves. I was *not* looking forward to being on a remote island with him.

Still, despite all my misgivings about my decision to

accept this offer, I couldn't help my curiosity about whatever was to come.

AS THE PLANE began its descent over the picturesque island, it finally hit me.

This was *real*.

Muzo clambered against the window. "Guys, look! It's a freaking island!"

Anxiety forgotten, Poppy glanced outside and gasped. "Oh, wow. It's beautiful."

Even I joined in. From the sky, I saw lush green forests, blue-gray mountains dotted with trees, and white sandy beaches. It looked like an award-winning photograph out of a nature magazine.

And we were going to live there for the foreseeable future.

The kind flight staff assured us our luggage would be brought to the hotel, so all we needed to do was walk there. After getting off the plane, we stepped out into the warm air. It was so clean and fresh, with a tinge of salt from the sea breeze. I closed my eyes to breathe it in. After the human city air, it smelled incredibly sweet and pure.

The hotel sat on a grassy outcropping above the beach. It was a modern building with clean lines. Despite being surrounded by untouched nature, it looked unobtrusive, like it was designed for minimal impact.

As we entered the lobby, I continued to be impressed. The inside of the hotel was modern yet homey, lavish yet unpretentious. It was nicer than any hotel I'd ever been in, but still managed to feel welcoming. Not like those glamorous rich people hotels I passed when walking downtown.

But in reality, we *were* competing for the affection of a

glamorous rich person—the unknown dragon brother. He was probably just as bad as those snooty humans. If so, he'd pick Alaric, who was already salivating to win.

After the concierge politely handed out key cards to our rooms, we were told to enjoy ourselves until the Games began that afternoon, when the opening ceremony was to be filmed. A mix of nerves and excitement fluttered in my stomach. I'd nearly forgotten that this whole spectacle was going to be broadcast on TV. I recalled the way Alaric riled me up earlier. I wouldn't let that kind of slip-up happen again, especially not for the world to see.

"Last one to their room loses!" Muzo declared before racing up the stairs.

"Loses what? You just made up a game on your own," I mumbled, following behind him at my own pace.

Poppy clutched his key card tightly. "Will they get mad if I lose this?"

"No, they won't," I promised. "If you do, they'll just give you another one." Seeing his uneasy expression, I said, "Nobody's out to get you here, Poppy. The staff and every-one's been nice to you so far, right?"

"Right..."

I smiled gently. "They *want* you to be here. That's why they invited you. So chin up."

"Okay."

Alaric scoffed as he briskly passed us. "You know some contestants get cast as filler, right? For there to be a winner, there have to be lots of losers. In fact, most of the people in this room are losers," he added with a smirk.

Poppy wilted. His shoulders slumped like a weight had dropped on them, and his big brown eyes filled with sadness.

Righteous anger filled me. It took everything I had not to claw Alaric's smug look off his face. Getting on my nerves was one thing, but harming Poppy's shaky confidence was something I would not tolerate.

"Leave my friend alone, Alaric," I growled. My tiger's voice rose to the surface, filling my throat with a rumbling vibration. I didn't realize how loud it was until multiple people turned to see. But this time, I didn't care. Getting stared at was worth it to defend my friend.

Alaric put his hands on his hips. "Or what? You're going to lunge at me? Claw me to shreds?"

Had he guessed I was a tiger already? Unlike him, I wasn't slathered in perfume, so it wasn't hard to miss my scent up close.

"I know you're trying to pick a fight with me, but leave Poppy out of it," I warned him.

"Some people just don't have the confidence to be a dragon's mate," Alaric said smoothly. "I'm just calling it as I see it."

His sudden shift in tone confused me. Why did it sound like he was speaking to an audience?

I caught motion in the corner of my eye. A short, scaly humanoid creature held up a big camera—and pointed it right at us.

Were they filming already?

The hairs on the back of my neck rose. Now I understood. Alaric had baited me on purpose. Again. And this time, he must've known the camera was nearby.

I wasn't in the mood to be filmed right now, but it was too late to back out. I'd already signed the contract to be recorded—whenever, wherever. Nowhere was truly private on this private island.

I put my hand on Poppy's shoulder. He'd frozen out of fear and needed help escaping the situation. Urging him away, I said, "Let's go, Poppy."

The short-legged, scaly creature briefly tried to catch

up with me—presumably to ask my opinion on what just happened—but I was much taller and faster, and escaped into the stairwell before he had the chance.

On the other hand, Alaric had no desire to dodge the spotlight. I heard him speaking loudly to the cameraman in an affected I-know-I'm-on-TV voice. I was shocked my eyes didn't pop out of my skull with how hard I rolled them.

I found Muzo on the second floor grinning like a maniac. He'd propped his front door open with his empty suitcase and gestured inside his new abode.

"Check it out," he said. "King bed. Private bathroom. Huge freaking windows with a view of the beach! And it's all *free!* Can you believe it?"

I had to admit, I was surprised at how gorgeous the room was, even with Muzo's things immediately strewn everywhere. It was easy to overlook the mess, though. The bright blue sky and crystal-clear waters were visually striking. The windows were more like glass walls that revealed a panoramic view of the island.

"Wow," I murmured.

Muzo laughed. "When Taylor's speechless, you know it's good." He blinked, then squinted at the window. "Hey, what's going on over there?"

All three of us shuffled against the glass. There was a commotion right outside the hotel. A crowd of those little scaly camera-wielding creatures huddled around a single figure, but respectfully kept their distance, as if the person was incredibly important.

My gaze focused on the figure. It was a tall man dressed in a brown suit. His jet-black hair was interrupted by a single blazing red streak. I couldn't see any other details from this distance, but he had a distracted and snooty aura, like he was uninterested in what was going on around him.

"Holy shit," Muzo muttered. "Do you think that's him? The dragon dude?"

My eyes widened. Could it be? If so, I was surprised Alaric hadn't slobbered on him already. But maybe he wasn't allowed to go near him yet, since the Games hadn't officially begun.

Suddenly, the man lifted his head.

He looked directly at me.

A tangible shock ran down my spine. Gasping, I backed away from the window.

What the hell was *that?*

I allowed myself a moment to get over the tingly sensation. Thankfully, neither of my friends noticed. They were both enthralled by the suit-wearing man outside.

"I'm gonna go to my room," I mumbled, then took off before they could stop me.

Once inside, I sighed loudly and collapsed on the bed. The crisp, white bed sheets felt cottony soft and comforting beneath my skin. I took a breath to decompress after the whirlwind chaos leading up to this point.

This was my new reality. I was a contestant in the Dragonfate Games. I'd entered on a whim, thinking it was to protect my friends... but was that really true?

Would my life be the same after this?

SIX

Crimson

_____

AS THE STAFF buzzed and bustled around, I did my best
not to yawn. Filming a TV show was a lot more boring
than I expected. Most of it involved waiting around while
the professionals did all the work. All I had to do was stand
there and look handsome. Easy enough.

But the opening ceremony was about to start, and
that's when my real work began. I had to act like I truly
gave a shit about the show and its contestants, if only to
pave the way for future seasons.

My brothers were counting on me, so I _guessed_ I'd give it
my all.

The ceremony was being filmed on the beach with the
sunset as a backdrop. A platform had been set up, and the
staff gathered the rested-up contestants from their rooms.

I glanced curiously back at the hotel. I hadn't seen the
omegas arrive, but I'd caught a glimpse of one through the
second-floor window. The sun's glare made it hard to tell
who it was, but I was oddly intrigued.

Not that it mattered. I wasn't bedding any of these
omegas. I just had to be friendly with them until this was

over. Maybe I'd throw in a round of flirting or two for good measure.

"You ready, bro?"

The dual voices came from behind me. Saffron and Aurum grinned expectantly. I was surprised to see them here so close to filming. Duke, the director, had told all my brothers to stay away from the set.

"Ready for this to end," I replied.

Aurum snorted. "Yeah, whatever. Once it starts, you'll change your tune."

"Doubtful."

"You're lucky," Saffron said, pouting. "We're not even allowed to watch the filming. We only get to show up at the end, after you find your mate. Duke says it'll warp our opinions on the contestants if they reappear on later seasons or something."

Duke currently barked last-minute orders on stage. He hadn't noticed them yet.

"Yeah, he put us in time-out and ordered us to stay put in the castle," Aurum grumbled.

As annoying as the twins were, I sensed their disappointment at not getting to watch.

"Think of it as delayed gratification for when you *do* finally get to meet the contestants," I reminded them. "Besides, you can watch the episodes after, right?"

Aurum frowned. "Yeah, but it's not the same..."

A bright voice called out, "Trouble in paradise, dragons?"

Gaius strolled over with a pearly white grin. He was a gryphon shifter, and a long-time friend of the family. With his oozing charisma and picture-perfect smile, he was the perfect host for the Games.

His cyan-blue Hawaiian shirt, on the other hand, was

my least favorite thing about him. It was an eye-searing abomination.

"Must you really wear that?" I asked with a sigh, pointing to the fashion atrocity.

Gaius let out a hearty laugh. "Crimson, come on! Everyone loves a Hawaiian shirt. It adds to the beach vibe."

"It makes me want to gag."

Gaius clapped me on the shoulder. "Gag over these sexy omegas instead. Some of them are smoking hot, my friend."

The twins snickered over the word *gag* and mumbled something about dicks.

"Better run, you two," Gaius warned. "Duke is coming this way."

Aurum and Saffron bolted just as the angry kobold stormed towards them, shaking his fist.

"Yeah, you run, dragon runts!" Duke shouted. "Damn kids... Are you two ready?"

"You bet, sir," Gaius replied cheerfully.

I sighed. "Ready as I'll ever be."

"Good." Duke snapped his fingers. "Omegas at the ready. Crimson, Gaius, on stage. Shooting starts in five."

Being ordered around by a kobold wasn't my idea of a good time, but I obediently followed Duke's orders. I figured I should be grateful that he knew what he was doing. He'd make this process go as smoothly and pain-lessly as possible.

"You're stiff," Gaius pointed out. "Loosen up, brother."

"Sure. Let me relax before I go on television to be gawked at by a bunch of lecherous, gold-digging omegas."

Gaius was completely unfazed by my comment. "It's going to be great! Look, here they come now."

A parade of men approached the filming area. The

staff had equipped them all with hidden microphones and given them directions.

Gaius excitedly scanned the new arrivals. "Aren't they all stunners? You could take your pick at random and still be happy."

"Appearances aren't everything," I mumbled.

"I bet they're all nice, too."

"Anyone can fake being nice."

Gaius chuckled. "Except you. Don't scare them away."

"I'm a dragon. We're *supposed* to be scary. Fire? Talons? Fangs? Any of that ring a bell?"

"Give it a chance, Crimson," Gaius said merrily. "You never know what life has in store."

I wished life would let me go home to my hoard, but I was stuck doing this instead.

Duke scowled at me from below the platform. "Smile like you mean it, Crimson! You look like an angsty teenager next to Gaius."

"Everybody looks like that next to him," I said.

Duke muttered some kobold curse under his breath.

Gaius didn't seem as bothered by my face. "You look great, brother. Handsome as usual."

Oddly enough, his compliment quelled some of my jitters. "Thanks, Gaius."

He flashed me a grin just before Duke's hand shot into the air.

"We're on in three... two..."

My heart flip-flopped.

But Gaius held no such anxiety. He shone like a beacon of charisma as he stepped forward on the stage. All eyes were on him as Duke's hand flew down. The filming had begun.

"Have you ever wondered what it would be like to date a dragon?" Gaius asked, grinning at the camera. "Well, now's your chance to find out. Ladies and gentlemen, lovely non-binary viewers, and everybody outside or in between—welcome to the very first Dragonfate Games! I'm your host, Gaius the gryphon, and I'll be leading you on this ground-breaking whirlwind adventure of love. Here on a beautiful private island, twenty omegas will compete for the grand prize—the love of a single alpha dragon."

Dear Drake, this was really happening, and *I* was the dragon Gaius spoke of. Were there really twenty contestants? I hadn't bothered counting because I had no interest in looking at them, but I couldn't pretend like they didn't exist anymore.

As Gaius introduced the audience to the show, I raked my gaze over the line of omegas. They'd all been fitted with microphones, the same as me. I couldn't believe twenty men had signed up for this experience willingly... except I could. They all wanted fame or fortune, nothing more. Since I could be on camera at any moment, I tamped down my bitterness as I looked at them.

None of them stood out to me—except one.

The tiger.

My breath caught in my throat when I saw him in the flesh. There he was, standing fifteen feet away. Broad-shouldered, powerful, stoic. He looked bigger in person, and he had a presence that the others lacked, a magnetic force. Try as I might, I couldn't look away from him.

And then he looked back.

Ferocious amber eyes locked on mine. In the golden light of the sunset, they looked like orbs of fire, hot and burning. He didn't blink. He stared—almost *glared*—like he had a bone to pick with me.

For a second, I lost all sense of time and place. I forgot about the film set, the staff, everyone on the beach, and hell, even the beach itself. All I knew was the blazing glare of the tiger omega before me.

Then Gaius clapped me hard on the shoulder, jerking my attention back to the here and now.

"—and they'll be competing for *this* alpha," Gaius said with a flashy grin. "Why don't you introduce yourself?"

Fuck. Brain cells. I had to use them.

I plastered on a smile. "Crimson Chromatimaeus. Nice to meet you all."

Gaius gave me an ever-so-slight raise of his brows, indicating I needed to say more.

Dammit, he made improv look so easy. What the hell was I supposed to say?

But then I imagined my brothers groaning at my abject failure on television. If nothing else, I'd power through it to prevent them from making fun of me later.

Injecting an ounce of sincerity into my smile, I said, "I've been without a mate for a long time, and I'm eagerly looking forward to finding him. I hope fate will bring us together during the Dragonfate Games."

The pleased look on Gaius's face told me that was exactly what he—and the audience—wanted to hear.

"You heard it straight from the dragon's mouth, folks," Gaius announced. "Now without further ado, let's watch our coveted alpha dragon mingle with the contestants for the very first time!"

Mingle? Oh, for the love of...

Gaius led me off stage towards the strip of sandy beach where the omegas stood. The camera crew circled around us like a pack of wolves, seizing every opportunity for footage. I fought off the urge to shift into my dragon form and thwack them away with my tail, but that was probably an OSHA violation.

A small table stood in the center. Pre-mixed drinks

were available for the omegas. Alcoholic, I presumed. Inebriated contestants made for better TV. The thought made me want to roll my eyes. Lowered inhibitions combined with desperation was a total turn-off.

I pushed my personal feelings aside and took a can of non-alcoholic cranberry soda. I liked the way the bubbles tickled my throat.

As I took a sip, I realized all the omegas were staring at me. It was clear they all wanted my attention, but none of them were brave enough to step forward and make the first move. I withheld a sigh. This felt more like an awkward high school dance than speed dating.

Gaius must have sensed my hesitation. He took the initiative to break the ice.

"Let's meet our contestants, shall we?" he said to the closest camera.

Before Gaius could pick someone at random, a slender white-haired omega stepped forward. His odd-colored eyes gleamed mischievously.

"Hello, Gaius," he said. "I'll introduce myself while I speak to Crimson, if that's okay."

Gaius nodded, waving for the camera to follow. "Of course, go right ahead."

Flashing a sultry smile, the white-haired omega took a sip from his straw while extending a hand to greet me. "Alaric."

"Crimson."

"I can see that." Alaric let out a soft laugh, glancing at the red streak in my hair. "Does the dragon match?"

"It does."

Excitement glimmered in his eyes. "Wow. I can imagine how big it is."

I wasn't stupid. I knew he was flirting with me. But it surprised me how much I didn't care for it. In the back of my mind, I'd worried my primitive alpha instincts would flare up at the first scent of an omega. Thankfully, that didn't happen. Maybe it was the overwhelming perfume Alaric wore, but I felt no desire to get closer to him.

This was TV, though. I had to be cordial.

I tried changing the subject. "What's your shifter animal?"

Alaric tilted his head, letting his white hair fall across his forehead. "You can't tell?"

I smiled politely. "I'm afraid to guess and get it wrong."

"You're a dragon." Alaric reached out and brushed his fingers against my arm. "I'm sure you're not afraid of *anything*."

My skin tingled unpleasantly. I subtly backed off from Alaric so I wasn't in his range, then pretended like I'd finished my drink. "Ah, empty already? Let me grab another."

I felt Alaric's disappointment like a tidal wave, but I didn't let it get to me. This was a competition, after all. He couldn't win in the first five minutes just by batting his eyelashes.

At the drink table, I guzzled the rest of my cranberry soda and grabbed another. Good grief. If this happened every time I interacted with a contestant, I'd have to piss all night long.

Gaius ran around cheerfully interviewing each omega. I was supposed to be the center of attention, but he did the majority of the mingling, which I appreciated.

I just wanted to get this over with. With a sigh, I turned around to throw myself back into the fray.

I promptly bumped into somebody.

And spilled my cranberry soda over us both.

My inner dragon shrieked. My suit. I got soda *all over my precious suit*. Any harm done to an item from my hoard was the worst crime imaginable. Still aware I was potentially being filmed, I did my best to quell my righteous draconic fury.

I scowled, ready to chew out the person I'd bumped into, until I saw who it was.

Taylor stood right next to me. His clean white shirt was *also* covered in spilled soda. His scowl matched mine, deep and disappointed.

But at the sight of him, something odd happened.

My fury dissipated. My dragon soul quieted without a peep. I suddenly didn't care about my suit. Which was utterly deranged, because I cared about my suits more than anything.

"Typically people apologize when they spill things on others," Taylor remarked dryly.

That was the first thing he ever said to me.

He was right, of course. But for some reason, I lacked the capacity to speak. My inner dragon had silenced his cries, but continued to stir restlessly.

Despite my internal floundering, I managed to sound normal. "I'm sorry."

"It's fine," Taylor said tonelessly. "I guess I own a pink shirt now."

I glanced at him up and down. With his previously white shirt, black pants, and cleanly combed hair, Taylor was well put together. He put effort into his appearance but didn't take it over the top. And thank Drake, he didn't reek of artificial perfume. The scent that wafted from him was natural and clean. I liked it.

Maybe a little too much.

I cleared my throat. "Crimson."

"Taylor."

"I know. I saw your file."

Taylor took a sip from his drink. "Good to know we're

on an even playing field."

The sarcasm dripping from his comment felt like a verbal backhand, yet it excited me. He wasn't rubbing against me like Alaric, or meekly watching me from afar like the other contestants. He had a spine.

I gestured to his glass. "Virgin?"

Taylor pointedly raised a brow.

Fuck me.

"The drink," I clarified. "Not you."

He kept holding my gaze. "Yes."

"You don't drink?" I asked.

"I don't like being in altered states of consciousness. Especially while I'm being filmed on a remote island with a bunch of strangers."

I smirked. "Isn't that what you signed up for?"

"Can't argue with that," he mumbled before taking another sip.

Taylor clearly wasn't thrilled to be here. He didn't even seem to give a shit that he was speaking to an alpha dragon. That intrigued me.

Among the crowd, I saw Alaric fuming. He made no effort to hide the contempt on his face as he glared a hole in the back of Taylor's head.

Two other men watched us intently. One grinned ear-to-ear, while the other looked on shyly.

"Friends of yours?" I asked, nodding to the pair.

Taylor's expression softened. "Yeah. They're the reason I'm here."

I blinked, taken aback, then laughed. "Ouch. What a blow to my ego."

"I couldn't care less about your ego," Taylor said mildly. How he uttered such a cruel statement in such an inoffensive and charming way, I had no clue. Before I could banter with him further, he asked, "Why don't you go talk to them instead?"

"You don't seem to understand how this works," I said playfully. "I'm the alpha dragon you're competing for. You're supposed to claw your way to the top for my affections."

Taylor shot a fierce glare my way, his burning eyes stabbing into me like shards of amber. It sent a shiver down my spine. I liked that he challenged me.

A doubt in the back of my mind flared up. What if this wasn't the real Taylor? Was he playing a game? I wondered if he'd adopted a thorny persona to stand out from the crowd. There was only one thing to do: spend more time with him and find out.

I half-expected him to insult me and storm off. Instead, he coolly picked up his drink and said, "Excuse me," leaving without fanfare.

Well, that certainly wasn't the dramatic TV moment it could've been. Maybe I'd read into Taylor's behavior too much. Whatever went on in his mind, it fascinated me.

Perhaps this experience wouldn't be all *that* bad.

SEVEN

Taylor

I COULDN'T SLEEP that night.

The hotel bed was clean, soft and comfortable. I was exhausted from the trip and all the mingling.

But that gods-damned dragon alpha wouldn't get out of my head. Every time I tried to think about something else, he'd pop back into my mind, forcing me to remember our interaction and his stupidly handsome face.

Crimson wasn't what I expected. Sure, he was still haughty and arrogant, but not quite as bad as I'd thought. For now. He'd get worse as the competition wore on and more of the omegas fawned and drooled over him, boosting his already-inflated ego...

The next morning, I ate a surprisingly good breakfast provided by the hotel staff and met the rest of the contestants in the lobby. I noticed the small, scaly cameramen tucked into the corners of the room, ready to film any drama. They mainly blended into the background, so it wasn't hard to ignore them.

Unlike me, my friends looked well-rested and ready to meet the day. Muzo bounced off the walls as usual, and

Poppy seemed in brighter spirits despite his ever-present anxiety.

I noticed the other omegas gave me a wide berth. Was it my size? I tried not to dwell on it too much.

"Morning, guys," I said.

Muzo wriggled his eyebrows. "Hey, Mr. Popular."

"Very funny."

"Hey, for once, I'm not joking. Did you know you held the longest conversation with Crimson yesterday?"

I stopped rubbing the sleep from my eyes. "What?"

Muzo huffed, crossing his arms. "He barely spent a second with me and Pops. Seriously, the guy speed-ran the rest of his meet-and-greets."

"I didn't know that," I said.

"Yeah, 'cause you went and sulked by the water after storming away from him."

I frowned in embarrassment. "I wasn't sulking. I just didn't want to talk to him anymore."

Muzo smirked and leaned in. "You should've seen Pretty Boy. He was freaking *pissed* that you spent so much time with Crimson!"

I assumed he meant Alaric.

"It was the other way around," I mumbled. "Crimson spent time with me. After spilling soda all over my white shirt, no less."

Alaric's voice suddenly blared out haughtily behind me. "You should be grateful that a dragon spilled *anything* on you."

"Why are you constantly manifesting in my private conversations?" I growled.

"First of all, they're not private. You're all mic'd and on television," Alaric sneered. "Second, you shouldn't even be here with that attitude, Taylor Chalchin."

I sneered back, raising my lip to reveal a not-yet-shifted

fang. "Don't say my full name. How do you even—never mind. Mind your own business, will you?"

Alaric didn't back off. "This *is* my business. I'm here to win, and you clearly aren't. So you should go home. That's all."

He strode off like he'd made a final grandiose statement.

I sighed. "What happened to him needing losers to be a winner?"

"Sheesh, that guy wakes up on the wrong side of the bed every single day." Muzo gasped. "Oh, look! It's the host!"

The whirring automatic door revealed Gaius, the gryphon shifter, and his camera crew entourage. He wore a new Hawaiian shirt—today it was sunny orange. He beamed a charismatic smile as he greeted us.

"Good morning, contestants! How was your first night at the hotel?" After a few people responded in various positive ways, Gaius went on. "Great, glad to hear it! Now, I'm excited to announce your very first challenge on the Dragonfate Games. It's time to ditch the clothes, because today you'll be competing in your shifter forms!"

A murmur of shock and excitement went up among the contestants.

"I'll tell you more when we reach the challenge area," Gaius said, winking. "Follow me."

The group trailed Gaius deeper into the island. It was our first time exploring anywhere except the beach right next to the hotel. The sand turned to earth beneath our feet as we entered a small forest. The canopy was sparse enough to see the sky above.

"Our shifter forms!" Muzo exclaimed, bouncing on his heels. "I'm so stoked. I haven't shifted since—well, I do it at home, duh—but never in public."

"We haven't forgotten," I assured him. "It's instinct."

I cast a curious glance at the rest of the omegas. What kind of shifters were they? I'd been friendly to the others in passing, but didn't make a serious effort to get to know them since they kept their distance from me. I noticed cliques had already started to form, with the big crowd splitting off into smaller ones, but one person was noticeably absent of any sort of friend group. Alaric walked by himself, speaking to nobody. I found that odd since he was so willing to insert himself into other people's business. I supposed everybody else found it as annoying as I did.

Gaius finally stopped beside a wide, rushing river. In the center was a small, grassy island. I paused when I saw Crimson standing there. Even from the side of the river, there was no mistaking that fancy suit and black-and-red hair.

I huffed at the sight of him. What made him so important?

Gaius raised his voice to be heard over the rushing water. "All right, omegas! Here we are at our first challenge. Your task is to cross this river and reach Crimson in the center. As a dragon, Crimson needs a mate who can keep up with him, through brains or brawn or something else entirely. There's no wrong way to win the challenges. Creativity is key!"

"Woohoo!" Muzo's voice overpowered his. "Finally, we're on a private island and we get to swim!"

Poppy fussed beside me. "We have to cross the river? The water looks fast..."

As a wolf, Poppy should've been a decent natural swimmer. But he was anxious about everything, including this. I put my hand on his shoulder comfortingly.

"I'll be right next to you. Don't worry," I said.

Poppy frowned. "But you should be trying to win. I'll slow you down if I can't keep up."

"I don't care about that."

That wasn't the whole truth. In the very back of my mind, I did care, for some strange reason. Maybe I was more competitive than I thought. But it was overpowered by my urge to protect my friend.

Gaius looked ready to start the challenge. "Any questions, omegas?"

"I've got one," Alaric announced. He stood at the river's edge, not yet shifted but clearly ready to go. "So the first contestant to reach the island—and Crimson—is the winner?"

"Not quite," Gaius said. "Any contestant who reaches Crimson has a *chance* to win. I'm sure plenty of you are strong and determined enough to make it across the river. Ultimately, it's his choice who wins."

Alaric looked slightly peeved. "All right. Then *if* Crimson chooses us, what do we win?"

Gaius grinned. "A dinner date with the dragon himself."

Alaric's eyes widened, flashing intently. It was obvious he'd do anything to win that date. I'd think he was pathetic if some secret part of me didn't also want to win.

"What happens if we don't make it to the center island?" Poppy asked.

Gaius gave him a warm, sympathetic glance. "Unfortunately, any contestants who don't complete the challenges will be disqualified."

Poppy's shoulders slumped. "Oh."

I hated seeing Poppy like that. Growling softly, I lowered myself to his eye level. "Hey. Don't give up when it hasn't even started yet."

"But the water's so choppy and fast, and I'm not the

best swimmer..." Poppy rubbed his arm. "If you and Muzo make it and I don't, they'll send me home. I'll be all alone..."

"You *will* make it," I assured him. "I won't let you be alone, Poppy."

He took a deep breath. My promise calmed him down a bit.

Alaric snorted. "If you need a pep talk on the very first challenge, you're not cut out to be a dragon's mate."

I held Poppy's gaze so he couldn't look at that asshole and give him the satisfaction of getting attention.

"Don't listen to him. He probably can't even doggy paddle." I smiled at Poppy. "But you can *wolf* paddle. Right?"

That earned a small smile back. "Yeah, I can do that."

"Good. Do it all the way there. Slow and steady, okay?"

Poppy nodded.

With my friend cheered up, I readied myself at the river's edge. Determination roared inside me. I'd show up that asshole Alaric *and* help Poppy to the finish line.

"Omegas!" Gaius called. "You may now shift!"

I took a deep breath and closed my eyes.

It was time to unleash my tiger.

Pure rippling power washed over me like a tidal wave. I let my human soul be swallowed up by the feral tiger roaring within me. My body twisted and reshaped itself in its image. When I opened my eyes, I stood on four huge paws. My long tail lashed like a whip. My curved, white claws flexed, gripping the earthy edge of the river.

With my sharpened eyesight, I glanced along the starting line. Beside me was a soft, fluffy Arctic wolf. Poppy.

Next to him was a smaller, pointier canine with tawny fur and a black back. Muzo's snout split in a toothy grin, the same as in his human form.

Beyond my two friends, I didn't recognize anybody. Except...

Standing off to the side was a haughty figure I'd recognize in any form. With pure white fur that matched his human form's hair, Alaric perched on the edge of the river as a domestic house cat. His perfectly groomed long fur was about to get ruined in the water.

No wonder he had such an attitude problem. His shifter form was tiny. I could've batted him around like a soccer ball with one paw.

I didn't have time to get a good look at the other shifters. The challenge was about to start.

Gaius raised his arm. "Ready, contestants? On three... One... two…"

With my sharp tiger eyes, I glared at Crimson. I could see him better in this form. He stood there with his hands tucked into his suit pockets like he was some great prize. What a joke.

And yet, I couldn't help the burning feeling in my chest that I wanted to win.

"GO!" Gaius yelled.

I leapt into the river. I didn't let the cold water slow me down. I paddled out with my powerful paws, letting my natural instincts take over. Tigers were gifted swimmers and I was no exception. Crossing the rushing waves came easily to me.

I didn't see anybody else. Was I in the lead?

I paused to glance over my shoulder.

Muzo was behind me, spitting water out of his mouth and paddling hard. His jackal form was small and he struggled in the river. "Argh, I hate swimming!"

"I thought you *wanted* to swim," I reminded him.

"Changed my mind," he grumbled. "Where's Poppy?"

We both looked behind us. A yellowy-white wolf

paddled slowly near the starting point. My heart sank. He'd barely made any progress, but at least he hadn't given up.

Muzo sighed. "Oh, Pops."

"You go ahead," I said. "I'll help him."

Muzo cocked his head. His wet, pointy ears flopped awkwardly. "You sure? You've got a huge lead on everyone else. You could be the first to the island."

"What do I care?" I grumbled. "If Poppy doesn't make it, then winning is worthless."

Muzo laughed. "You're a funny guy, Tay."

I splashed water at him with my paw. He knew I hated that nickname. "Get out of here, you annoying hyena."

"I'm a *jackal*!" Muzo called back as he swam away.

Turning around, I headed back to meet Poppy. Unfortunately, I ran right into Alaric, who'd managed to keep pace. The tiny cat was soaked to the bone, but surprisingly, he didn't look as miserable as I expected him to.

He *did* glare furiously at me, though.

"What are you doing?" Alaric hissed.

"Going to Blockbuster. What does it look like I'm doing?"

That angered Alaric. "Helping your sad little friend won't help you win. If you were smart, you'd turn around and swim to the island."

"Then I guess I'm not as smart as you."

I didn't wait around to hear Alaric's retort. Flicking my tail dismissively, I swam back to my friend. Poppy's ears were flat against his head and his lips were pulled back into an anxious grimace. His wolf paddling hadn't gotten him far.

He whimpered when he saw me. "Taylor? What are you doing here?"

"Funny. Alaric just asked me the same question." I pressed my body weight against his. "Grab onto me."

"But... is that against the rules?" Poppy asked nervously.

"Gaius didn't say we couldn't help each other," I replied. "And if I'm breaking some hidden rule, then so be it. Come on, we're wasting daylight."

Poppy hesitated, then gently grabbed the loose scruff of my neck with his teeth. I shot forward.

It took no time at all to reach the front of the pack again. Though, I was focused on getting ahead, I noticed the shifters around me. Deer, foxes, bears, and various other species I couldn't pick out over the waves. None of them could outpace me. My strong paws and powerful muscles put me in the lead once more.

Actually, I *would've* been in the lead, but there was one more person in front of me—a soggy-wet cat pushing himself to the limit. I was honestly surprised to see Alaric beating the rest. Maybe he wasn't as much of a fragile twink as he looked like.

Alaric was centered on winning. He didn't realize I gained on him until it was too late. He did a double-take and hissed loudly.

"When did *you* get back here?" Venom dripped from his voice.

"Just now," I replied.

Without waiting, I pushed on ahead. I felt Alaric's radiating fury behind me like swarming black tentacles.

But he was a house cat and I was a tiger. There was no competition in a physical race.

The shore of the little island was a few strokes away. With one final push, I leapt onto the strip of land. After Poppy detached from my scruff, I shook out my pelt and instinctively licked the water from my paws. Being in the water was fine, but being wet on dry land afterwards was *ugh*.

I felt somebody's burning gaze on me, but for once, it wasn't Alaric and his rage-filled, odd eyes. It came from above. I lifted my head.

In the center of the island, the tall man in a suit stood on the edge of the hill looking down at me. The alpha dragon.

Crimson.

A wave of irritation washed over me. My claws sank into the dirt. This river-crossing charade was all his fault. The guy was deranged for making omegas compete against each other like this.

Then again, I agreed to be on this idiotic game show, so maybe I was deranged, too.

As I locked eyes with Crimson, I glared at him. He met my gaze without blinking. I couldn't read his expression. He didn't seem particularly thrilled or displeased.

"He's staring right at you," Poppy murmured.

I flicked my tail crossly. "Let him."

Heavy wing beats sounded above us. A half-eagle, half-lion creature landed beside Crimson, then shifted into a cheerful man in an eye-searing Hawaiian shirt.

Gaius gestured theatrically down to the shore. "And we have our first arrivals! Poppy the Arctic wolf, and Taylor the Siberian tiger!"

A shiver went down my spine. For a moment, I'd forgotten this was all being filmed. I tried not to look *too* pissed off. But deep down, I was glad not to be disqualified. I didn't understand why, but I desperately wanted to win.

I chalked it up to my protectiveness over Poppy and Muzo. I couldn't look after them if I went home, right?

As I thought of my jackal friend, I glanced behind me. I sighed in relief when I saw him doggy-paddling his way to the shore, spitting out water. He'd made it to the next round, too.

And he wasn't alone. A dripping-wet white furball clawed his way onto the island. If my glare at Crimson was bad, Alaric's glare towards me was ten times worse. I was sure I'd be on the receiving end of his harsh words later.

"And two more contestants have just arrived," Gaius announced. "Muzo the black-backed jackal, and Alaric the cat! Ah, and a few more are right on their tails!"

A couple more stragglers wound up on shore. Soon a dozen shifters stood there, wet and waiting for Crimson to announce the ultimate winner. A few shifters were unable to swim to the island and bowed out of the competition, which only served to annoy me further. Crimson thought he was too good for people who couldn't swim? What a dick.

Muzo smacked his lips next to me. "Bleh, I swallowed a pound of seaweed..."

"We were in a river, there was no seaweed," I grumbled.

Poppy sheepishly licked Muzo's damp ears to dry them off. I ignored my canine friends. All my attention was on Gaius as he wrapped up his announcement of the contestants still in the running.

"That's everyone, folks! Congratulations on passing your first challenge. You've all won a chance at a date with Crimson tonight, but the final decision is his to make. I'll hand it over to the big man himself."

Gaius gave Crimson the microphone. Crimson looked slightly dazed. He distractedly brought it to his lips but didn't speak.

"Well, Crimson?" Gaius prompted in an upbeat tone. "Which omega will it be?"

Crimson glanced over the line of wet omegas. He

didn't spare any of them a lingering glance—except for me.

My heart suddenly began pounding.

Why was my body reacting? I didn't give a damn about this stupid competition. I couldn't care less if I won or lost.

But as Crimson's ruby eyes dawdled on me, my pulse picked up speed.

Finally, Crimson opened his mouth.

"The winner of this challenge, and the omega I choose to take on a date tonight... is Taylor Chalchin."

EIGHT

Crimson

PERHAPS I SHOULD'VE PAID MORE attention during the planning stage of the Dragonfate Games, because I surely would've spoken up about the utterly ridiculous "challenges" my brothers had thought up. Honestly, asking omegas to shift and swim across a river? Who came up with this nonsense? The worst part was that I was positive *every* challenge would be as idiotic as this one.

After the producers propped me up on the island in the middle of the river, I had no choice but to stand there and watch the water race. I didn't give a kobold's ass if my potential mate could swim across rushing waters. I mean, really, when was that ever going to be an issue? I'd rather my mate be challenged in dry cleaning or sewing in order to maintain my suits...

Apparently, those activities didn't make good television. None of it was up to me except the final choice of the winner—and in this case, there was no contest. I'd had my eye on Taylor since the meet-and-greet when he gave me the cold shoulder, and I'd been drawn to his photo before filming even began. There was something about that stoic tiger that intrigued me.

When the challenge started, Taylor had instantly taken the lead. It made sense. Tigers were excellent swimmers. I was secretly pleased he'd make it to the front of the pack.

But then he turned around.

At first, I couldn't comprehend what he was doing. Was he giving up? Was he doing the challenge all wrong just to spite me?

Then it dawned on me. He turned around to help his struggling friend.

That's what made my heart skip a beat. Taylor had a huge head start and an incredible advantage. He could've beaten the crowd and come in first place with plenty of time to spare. Instead, he'd aided someone in need. I didn't see that kind of compassion every day, especially not on a reality TV show.

When Taylor arrived on the shore with his wolf friend, I couldn't help but stare at him. He enthralled me. He was something special.

And what did I get from staring at Taylor?

A furious glare back from the sassy tiger.

I couldn't help but be amused. Even his thorny side was endearing.

It felt like an eternity before the final line of omegas appeared before me. I already had my choice. When Gaius handed me the mic, I was relieved for this to be over.

"The winner of this challenge, and the omega I choose to take on a date tonight... is Taylor Chalchin."

Taylor's eyes widened. For a split second, the righteous fury in his eyes vanished, replaced by pure shock—and maybe something else—but then the irritated glare returned with a vengeance.

And speaking of vengeance, that white cat shifter Alaric looked ready to go on the warpath.

That was none of my concern. I only wanted to know what Taylor was thinking.

Gaius leapt down to shore, ready to carry on with the production. "Congratulations, Taylor! You've won the honor of dining with Crimson tonight. How do you feel?"

He thrust the mic at Taylor, who looked too shocked to respond. A million cameras were trained on him, along with the eyes of every omega who'd lost to him. I felt empathy for Taylor. He wasn't the type to bask in the spotlight. Just like me. Maybe that's why I felt a connection with him.

"I... I don't know," Taylor mumbled.

Gaius laughed good-naturedly. "That surprised, eh? Don't worry, Crimson doesn't bite. Unless you ask."

My jaw dropped as Gaius winked. That bird brain...

Taylor didn't respond to the teasing joke. He didn't even give a polite chuckle.

But Gaius was a champion showman and didn't let the brief lull become awkward. "Good luck tonight, Taylor! And great job to the rest of our contestants. You're still in the running to win the Dragonfate Games—and Crimson's heart."

I saw Alaric's eyes flash hungrily. He was a cute omega, but the ravenous desperation wasn't my thing. I wasn't looking forward to turning him down.

What I *was* looking forward to was my date with Taylor. After Gaius's announcement wrapped up, I eagerly headed down the hill to talk to Taylor. But before I could even get close, Gaius grabbed my arm and shuffled me away.

"What are you doing?" I demanded.

He shot me a sorry look. "No can do, drago."

I hated that stupid nickname. "And why not?"

"We need tension for the cameras. Keeping you two apart until your date builds drama."

A growl slipped from my teeth. "I don't care about drama. Let me speak to him."

"C'mon, Crimson. Duke will have my tail feathers."

I tried to sidestep around him. "You can afford to lose a feather or two."

Gaius gripped me tighter. Bird brain or not, he was still a gryphon and had the strength of a mythical beast the same as I did.

"Weren't you listening during the million briefings?" Gaius sighed. "Just because this is a fun game show to find your mate, you still have to follow the rules."

"I think we have a different definition of fun," I said sourly.

Gaius smiled and patted my upper chest. "Your date's only a few hours away. Relax for a while. Have a drink or two beforehand. It'll be time before you know it."

I was about to argue with him when I realized what I was doing. Wasn't I vehemently against this whole concept in the first place? Now I was almost *begging* Gaius to go let me talk to a contestant?

I reeled myself back. I wasn't an out-of-control heathen. I could wait.

"Fine," I grumbled.

"YOU LIKE HIM! YOU LIKE HIM!"

I rubbed my temples. Returning to the castle was a mistake. Saffron and Aurum danced around me like a pair of cackling hyenas. They wouldn't shut up about my apparently obvious crush on Taylor.

"Of course I like him, that's why I chose him to win the challenge," I snarked back. "That doesn't mean anything."

Aurum's grin went from ear to ear. "Yeah, but you *like* him."

"What an astute observation of what I literally just said."

"Are you getting attached yet?" Saffron asked, leaning on the table.

"I barely know him," I said. "Now go bother someone else."

It was no use. The golden twins were glued to me in their mission to squeeze out every possible bit of gossip.

"Never thought of you as the type of dragon to fall for a cat," Aurum teased.

"Taylor is not a cat. He's a tiger."

"Um, tigers *are* cats, genius."

Saffron looked smug. "Crimson's making a distinction because he doesn't like that white cat, Alaric."

Oh, dear. Was it that obvious?

"I don't dislike him. He's simply not my type," I said.

Aurum nudged me. "Yeah, you like 'em big and strong, with broad shoulders and a moody face."

"Taylor does not have a moody face," I argued. "He's... stoic."

"Yeah, he's so stoic that it looks like he doesn't even *want* to go on a date with you!"

The way my stomach flipped at that statement was embarrassing. What if Aurum was right? What if, for some reason, Taylor didn't want to be here at all? Had I just roped him into an uncomfortable situation?

No, that couldn't be right. If that was how he truly felt, he could've lost on purpose, or withdrawn from the Games outright. Something kept him here.

What was it?

NINE

Taylor

_____

"YOU MISSED A SPOT. HERE."

I ruffled the clean towel behind Poppy's neck, under a patch of pale blond hair.

After the challenge, all the omegas had returned to the hotel to get changed. The ones who'd lost the challenge had already packed up and left. The rest of us who remained either roamed the beach by the hotel, sulking in our rooms after losing, or in my case, hung out with my friends until we dried off.

"Ah, thanks," Poppy murmured.

Muzo flopped on the bed with a loud sigh. "What a crazy challenge! Talk about a workout..." He suddenly sat upright, as if struck by a conspiracy. "What if that was secretly a challenge to find out how fit you are? Y'know, like how long you can have sex?"

I raised an eyebrow silently at him.

"Okay, fine, maybe not," Muzo admitted. "It just helps is all I'm saying. So, you excited for your big date?"

"Don't remind me," I mumbled.

"You're so weird. You just won a _date_ with a _dragon._

Literally anybody else would be pissing with excitement or nerves."

"My bladder is empty."

Now that Poppy was dry, I folded the used towel and put it away. When I got back from the bathroom, both my friends looked expectantly at me.

"What?" I asked.

"You don't have to spill to Gaius, but at least tell *us*, man," Muzo said. "We're your friends."

Poppy nodded. "You're not scared, are you?"

Dammit. If anyone could weasel something out of me, it was Poppy and his big puppy-dog eyes.

Sighing, I sat down on the bed next to them. "No. I'm not scared. I don't know what to feel, honestly."

Muzo and Poppy exchanged a curious glance.

"Are you happy?" Poppy asked softly.

I hesitated. Was I happy to go on a date with a pompous, arrogant alpha dragon who had organized a ridiculous dating show?

Well...

Maybe a little.

When I didn't respond immediately, Muzo barked out a cackle of laughter. "Holy shit. You *are* excited for this date!"

"N-no, I'm not," I grumbled.

He grinned. "No use lying to me. I see right through you, my man."

I got up abruptly from the bed. "I'm going to get a snack from the lobby."

My attempt to shake him loose didn't work. Muzo and Poppy trailed behind me as I waited for the elevator.

Muzo mimed holding a microphone to me. "Mister Chalchin, how does it feel to go on the first-ever date with Crimson?"

I mimed chucking the microphone thirty feet down the hall.

"Hey!" he cried.

The elevator doors opened—and revealed the last person I wanted to see. Alaric already looked annoyed before he recognized me, but when we stepped inside the elevator, he was ready to explode.

"Oh. It's *you*," he snipped.

I stared at the closing doors without looking at him. "Don't worry, the feeling's mutual."

But Alaric clearly wasn't in the mood to leave me alone. A hiss built in his throat. "You think you're such hot shit, don't you?"

"Stop projecting on me."

"I know your type," Alaric spat. "You exotic apex shifters are all the same, thinking you're better than the rest of us."

As much as I wanted to ignore the bait, the hairs rose on the back of my neck. Unfortunately, Alaric was skilled at getting on my nerves.

"I've never said that," I growled back. "Don't put words in my mouth, Alaric."

He rolled his odd-colored eyes. "Wow, the great tiger even knows my name."

Why wouldn't he leave me alone?

I'd had enough of this shit. I turned to him and asked, "What's your problem?"

"You," Alaric said flatly.

"What have I ever done to you?"

Alaric glared furiously at me. "You think you're too good for Crimson. I don't even know why you're here when you're obviously not taking the Dragonfate Games seriously."

I snorted. "If anyone's taking the *Games* too seriously, it's you."

An angry caterwaul rumbled in Alaric's throat. If he was in cat form, his white pelt would be spiked.

"Unlike you, I'm here to find a mate!" he snarled. "I'll prove my worth to Crimson. I'll show him I'm better than the riff-raff."

"Did you just call me riff-raff?"

Alaric's narrowed eyes glinted like knives. "It's what you are for toying with Crimson's heart."

Out of all the insults he'd hurled at me, that one cut me the deepest. The hairs rose on the back of my neck and my hands curled into fists at my sides.

"Don't make assumptions about me, *house cat*," I growled in a low voice.

Even Muzo must've felt the tension in the air because he thrust himself between us before a catfight began in earnest. In one breath, he said, "Hey, would ya look at that? We're in the main lobby already! Better get going, see you!"

Alaric remained in the elevator out of spite as the three of us emptied into the lobby.

I breathed a sigh of relief. "Sorry you guys had to see that."

Muzo patted me. "No worries, Tay. That twink has a chip on his shoulder. Let's grab a snack and relax before your big date. Ooh, speaking of chips, they have salt and vinegar..."

AS EVENING DESCENDED upon the island, my nerves were shot. I didn't particularly want to go on my date with

Crimson, but I also didn't *not* want to... It didn't make any sense.

I'd dressed in a simple white button-up shirt and black pants. Thankfully I had a spare shirt after Crimson dumped his drink all over the other one.

An unbidden snort of soft laughter came out of me at the memory. He was an idiot, yet still managed to be charming.

As I left the lobby, my friends wished me luck. Muzo had tried scrounging for a pair of binoculars so he could watch my and Crimson's ocean-side date from his hotel room, but couldn't find any. He'd have to be satisfied using his imagination.

I wasn't alone on the way to my date, though. An entourage of cameras followed me. The short, scaly camera crew—all lizard-people called kobolds—were good at staying out of sight, but that didn't stop the feeling of *knowing* I was being watched. Could I really enjoy a date while it was being filmed?

It was too late to do anything about it now. I'd sealed my fate the second I agreed to be on this foolish show.

The ocean breeze caressed my face, cool and salty. Ahead lay a sandy strip of beach with a wooden platform, the same one I'd seen in the opening ceremony. Warm lights and colored paper balls were strung around the perimeter, giving the space an inviting glow. A single table with two chairs stood in the center.

And there was Crimson.

As soon as he saw me, he stood up.

My heart fluttered oddly. It wasn't like me to get so nervous. It must've been all the cameras.

I stepped up onto the platform, trying not to notice the thickness in my throat or my uneven heartbeat. But I wasn't about to bow my head and defer to some cocky alpha. I held my chin high and met Crimson's ruby gaze straight on.

"Good evening, Taylor," he said with a smile.

"Evening."

He gestured to the chair opposite him. "Have a seat."

As we both sat, my eyes roamed across Crimson. He wore a different suit tonight, a striking blood-red blazer with a black pullover and matching red tie. I couldn't lie, he pulled off suits better than anyone I'd ever seen. He was smoking hot.

A sharply dressed waiter came by to silently deliver a menu and water. I noticed he didn't hand a menu to Crimson.

"You're not eating?" I asked.

He gave me a coy smile. "How sweet. Are you worried about me?"

I arched a brow. Annoying handsome bastard.

"Not so much worried as confused," I said.

He shrugged. "I don't need a menu when I know it all by heart. It's the typical dinner fare the staff serve at the castle."

I snorted, then looked down at the menu so I didn't have to meet his intriguing ruby eyes anymore. "Of course you're a dragon and live in a castle."

"Where did you expect me to live? In a shack?"

"No, I just shouldn't have expected a dragon to have so little humility."

He sounded amused. "You wound me. Are you always so cold to your dates?"

"I don't date," I said bluntly.

Crimson tilted his head, pausing for a second. He fingered the stem of his water glass. "And yet, here you are."

"I didn't ask to be chosen as the winner of your little challenge."

"True," Crimson conceded. "But you *did* ask to be part of the—" He paused, then sighed as if saying the next words physically pained him. "—Dragonfate Games, did you not?"

I looked back up at him. "Actually, I didn't. My friend tricked me into entering my name."

Crimson's brows shot up in surprise. Then he let out a soft, genuine laugh. "I see."

"What's funny?"

He circled his finger around the rim of his glass. "This whole charade wasn't my idea, you know."

"What do you mean?"

"My lizard-brained brothers put me up to it." Crimson smiled at me in a peculiar way, like we shared an inside joke. "I wanted nothing to do with the dating show. In fact, I vehemently shot the idea down... only to be outvoted."

I blinked at him. That wasn't what I expected, so I didn't know what to say.

"Oh," I said.

Crimson grinned, flashing his perfectly white teeth. "Really, Taylor. You think a man of taste like myself would desire a gaudy game show like this?"

From the corner of my eye, I saw one of the kobolds— the director, I thought—give Crimson the middle finger.

I lowered my voice. "Are you sure you should say things like that on camera?"

As if playing a game with me, Crimson leaned in and lowered his voice to match mine. "I'm a dragon, Taylor. This is my home. I can say and do whatever I want."

Something about the way he said that sent a shiver down my spine.

In a regular tone, he added, "Oh, and by the way, the

microphones are *very* high quality. They pick up whispers just as well as shouts."

I blushed slightly and pulled back. "Good to know," I mumbled.

When the waiter swung back around, we put in our food orders. He also dropped off a bubbly red drink for Crimson, and a fresh water for me.

"Sparkling wine?" I asked.

"Not quite. Something a little... closer to your heart."

I didn't get what he meant until I remembered my pink shirt. "Ah. Cranberry soda."

"That's right. I can get that shirt dry cleaned for you, by the way."

I shrugged. "It's fine. It's not normally my color, but I kind of like it pink now."

"Nonsense. Any color would look good on you."

Was he flirting with me or just being nice? I couldn't tell. Dodging his comment, I took a sip of my water.

"No wine for you, either," Crimson commented. "I recall you saying you don't drink."

"You remembered."

He smirked. "Yes. Even though you didn't remember my taste for cranberry soda."

I gave him a half-smile. "Sorry, I don't go around remembering every dragon's favorite soft drink."

A flicker of something—jealousy?—flashed across Crimson's eyes.

"You know other dragons?" he asked.

"No. You're the first I've met."

That seemed to calm him down. "Ah."

The waiter brought our food. I ordered a light meal so I didn't pig out on TV. The savory melted cheese crepe was doused in a creamy mushroom sauce, making my mouth water. Crimson's dish was a seared fish steak, likely fresh from the ocean. The tiger within me licked his lips at the scent of grilled flesh.

"Smells amazing," I said looking at his plate.

Without missing a beat, Crimson sliced a piece of his fish and offered it to me. I froze. He didn't put it on my plate—he expected me to take it straight from his fork.

Which meant putting my mouth on it. Which he would then put in his *own* mouth.

Crimson expectantly arched a brow, radiating smug energy. That asshole. He knew we'd be indirectly kissing on film.

The longer I hesitated, the dumber I felt. An indirect kiss? What was I, a teenager? What did it matter if we ate from the same fork? We were two adult men on a date, for gods' sake.

I bit down on his fork, then sat back. The smoky flavor of fish exploded on my tongue. It smelled good, but I didn't expect it to taste *that* incredible. Without thinking, I let out a small moan.

Shit.

Crimson's eyes widened. A glassy hungriness shone in them—and it wasn't directed at the food.

A flushed sensation shot through my body. I took a long gulp of icy water to cool off, but it didn't help.

"Thanks, I'm good," I mumbled, indicating I didn't want any more of his fish. I wouldn't be able to handle it if he offered again.

Crimson cleared his throat. "If you say so."

That was the end of it. Or, so I hoped.

Because a second later, something touched my foot under the table. It was Crimson's shoe.

A hot blush bloomed across my cheeks. What was that asshole thinking? Trying to make him stop, I nudged his foot back hard.

But Crimson just grinned. He thought I was playing with him. He circled my foot with his in a teasing gesture.

An electric jolt tingled my skin. I wanted to pull my foot away from him, but I couldn't bring myself to do it.

It felt... good.

Gods, what was I thinking? I must've been touch starved. I shouldn't have been so desperate that playing footsie under the table would get me so worked up.

I tried to ignore Crimson by eating my food. The crepe was just as delicious as it smelled. I'd never eaten something so divine. Now, though, I was careful *not* to moan embarrassingly about it.

"Sure you don't want another bite?" Crimson asked when I was finished. A hearty chunk of grilled fish remained on his plate.

Since I'd eaten light, there *was* room in my stomach... but if that meant subjecting myself to his cute-yet-annoying fork feeding, did I really want it?

My inner tiger growled. Yes, he did.

"Fine," I grumbled.

Looking delighted, Crimson offered me another piece. I took it. He didn't even bother to hide his joy as I swallowed. He liked feeding me.

That was kind of sweet, honestly.

We repeated the process until his plate was empty. I licked my lips, swallowing the last of the grilled fish juices. Now I felt truly satisfied.

Crimson regarded me fondly. "Has anyone ever told you how cute you are when you eat?"

My cheeks turned hot at the sudden comment. "W-what?"

"You get this eager, yet peaceful expression. It's very endearing."

My temperature skyrocketed. I was so baffled I didn't know how to respond.

"Um," I said. "Thanks?"

Crimson's shoe grazed against mine again. I shivered.

"No problem," he murmured, still gazing at me.

My heart flip-flopped in my chest. He *was* flirting with me. Nobody ever did that. Since I had no experience with it, I didn't know what to do except sit there silently, gawking at him.

Crimson tilted his head. "I guess the answer is no. I'm the first one to compliment you like this?"

I nodded slowly.

He grinned, clearly pleased. "When was the last time you were on a date, Taylor?"

The question made me bristle from bad memories. "It's ancient history."

"Really?" Crimson asked. His hand inched closer to mine across the table. "I can't imagine why a handsome tiger like yourself wouldn't be in high demand."

I felt my heart pounding in my throat. Where did all these compliments come from? Was he trying to put me on edge? Was this another game, another challenge?

"I don't know," I mumbled.

Crimson's eyes pierced mine. Those glinting ruby shards were impossible to break away from. They sucked me in, demanding my attention. Was this an alpha dragon's power?

I suddenly remembered the airplane pilot mentioning magic. That put a damper on my heightened feelings.

"You're using magic on me, aren't you?" I asked cynically.

Crimson frowned hard, his brows knitting together. "I would *never* do such a thing."

Hearing that I'd genuinely offended him made me feel guilty. "I'm sorry. That was rude of me."

Thankfully, he got over it quickly, returning to his previous teasing demeanor.

"That's all right," Crimson said. In a soft, alluring voice, he added, "Besides, I don't need magic to win you over, Taylor."

My heart fluttered like a trapped butterfly. I wasn't used to this flustered sensation. My skin felt hot and tingly, and it was harder to breathe than usual.

After the waiter cleared our table, Crimson stood. He offered me a hand to get up. Normally I would've refused, but I felt woozy and didn't trust my knees. I took his hand. It was warm and softer than I'd imagined.

"Thank you for a wonderful evening," Crimson said. I could tell he meant every word sincerely.

"You're welcome. I should thank you."

He looked pleased, which was oddly cute. Maybe I could afford to be less of a sourpuss towards him.

I noticed he was still holding my hand. I didn't bother to move it. He didn't, either. My pulse flickered. Crap. We held hands for so long that my palm was sweaty.

"Guess I should head back," I mumbled, retracting my hand.

"Mm."

Neither of us made a move to leave. My skin tingled where we'd touched, a phantom sensation left behind.

A thought came to me like a sudden lightning strike, powerful and searing-hot, scorching my mind: I wanted more of Crimson.

My cheeks flushed with heat. I turned around.

"I guess I'll see you tomorrow," I said.

I heard the tiniest crumb of disappointment in his voice. "Yes. Tomorrow."

As I got off the platform, I felt a gnawing resentment towards the cameras. I knew I'd signed up for constant filming, but it got old fast. I wished they weren't there, tracking my every move. It was invasive, but hey, wasn't that the point of a reality TV show? I'd made the choice to be filmed. Now I had to live with it.

But because of the cameras, I couldn't be fully authentic with Crimson. I remembered Alaric's goading, and how he played to the cameras. I wasn't like that. I was already a reserved person, and having lenses thrust in my face only made me want to retreat deeper into my stoic shell.

I just wanted a moment alone with Crimson. *Truly* alone. Maybe then I could untangle these weird feelings I had towards him...

Was that too much to ask?

TEN

Crimson

I DESPERATELY HOPED SITTING behind a table during dinner blocked my raging erection from the camera.

That was *not* the reaction I expected from myself. What began as a pleasant, if playful, evening with Taylor had turned into a battle of wills—my brain against my body.

And my brain lost by a landslide.

Nudging his foot beneath the table, caressing his hand —all those small, innocent touches were gasoline on a fire. My initial attraction to Taylor exploded. I craved him in a way I'd never experienced before.

It was shocking, honestly.

That final moment where the two of us hesitated to part filled me with budding hope. Did Taylor feel the same way I did?

As the date died down and the cameras turned off, I heaved a sigh of relief. What a chore. I couldn't wait for this reality TV nonsense to end.

But if it did, would I lose Taylor forever? Would he go home, back to his normal life, and leave me behind?

The idea terrified me. My inner dragon growled with

deep displeasure. I had to bite down on my cheek to stop myself from shifting in rage and despair.

Oh, Holy Drake, I was already too deep into this...

After Duke assured me filming was wrapped for the day, I stormed silently off set. I disappeared deep into the forest and shifted. My beloved suit was enchanted, and was safely swallowed up into my dragon's scales. Power rippled across my body, freeing me from my human form. My claws dug into the ground and I hissed in frustration.

Taylor.

I needed him.

A growl reverberated in my long throat. I didn't normally feel so... feral. I prided myself on controlling my draconic urges.

But Taylor had unlocked something within me, and now the beast couldn't be shoved back into its cage.

I paced the forest floor restlessly. What I *should've* done was gone back to the castle, slipped into my room and rested for tomorrow's filming. If today was any indication, the next day would be filled with similar nonsense.

But I was painfully awake, a crackling live wire. I couldn't have fallen asleep even if my eyes were duct-taped shut.

As the moon slowly rose, I spent an hour warring against my urges. It was nighttime. By now all the kobold staff must've gone home. The beach was dark and empty.

Which meant nobody would see me if I went to visit Taylor.

Dragons were impatient creatures who wanted what they wanted, and they wanted it *now*.

And I wanted Taylor right this second.

A switch flipped. My impulsive, reckless dragon side took over. Without sparing it another thought, I leapt into the sky and flew towards the omegas' hotel.

I recalled perfectly which room was his. I'd never forget after I locked eyes with him on his first day.

Now the question was—would he actually let me in?

I angled my wings, careful to stay quiet as I banked towards his room. When I reached the balcony, I hovered on top of it for a second, shifted in mid-air, then landed on the concrete ledge.

I blew out a breath and dusted off my suit. I caught my reflection in the glass. I still looked fantastic.

The inside of the room was dark. Looking closer, I noticed the curtains were drawn. What a shame. I would've liked to catch a glimpse of Taylor's sleeping form. I was sure it was adorable.

Would it be too creepy to open the sliding door and walk in?

Probably.

As much as my dragon soul wanted to claim Taylor right this second, I had to keep *some* decorum.

Instead of barging in like I wanted to, I knocked softly on the glass.

Quick footsteps were followed by the curtain being yanked aside. I stood face-to-face with a shocked Taylor. He gawked at me, dazed, like he wasn't sure if he was dreaming or not.

"Crimson?"

"Good evening."

He blinked rapidly, then hissed under his breath, "What the hell are you doing here?"

I pouted. "I thought you'd be happier to see me."

Taylor's bristling softened. He sighed. "I... I'm not *unhappy* to see you."

That brightened my spirits. "Really?"

"Yes. I'm just surprised." Taylor crossed his arms, but

he didn't look displeased. "You're not supposed to be here, are you?"

"Not at all," I said brightly.

Taylor snorted. "Figures. Alpha dragons can do whatever they want, right?"

There was no malice in his voice. He teased me in his usual stoic way.

"Funny you say that," I remarked. "Originally I was going to simply come inside, but I figured it was polite to knock."

"Oh, good. He has manners."

Despite the barbed sarcasm, I heard a hint of gentle amusement. He liked that I was here.

I sauntered closer. As I ate up the distance between us, Taylor didn't back away. He held his ground, eyes locking with mine. The sharp glint in his gaze reminded me that he was no pushover, either. He was a ferocious tiger—an apex predator just like me.

"Did you come here just to bother me?" Taylor asked. Again, no malice. It felt like he was being playful.

"Maybe," I teased. "Is that all right?"

"I don't have a choice, do I?"

"Sure you do. Tell me to leave, and I'm gone."

Taylor hesitated. Eventually he sighed like I was some big bother, but he said, "Fine. Stay. Not like I'm doing anything important."

As he said that, he glanced at the bed. I noticed a sheet of blue fabric on top of the hotel covers, along with a notebook scrawled with measurements.

"What's that?" I asked.

Taylor bristled. I felt his walls come back up, but I didn't understand why.

"I genuinely want to know, Taylor," I encouraged.

"Just my quilting," he mumbled.

My brows rose. "You quilt?"

"Yeah. It's not a big deal."

I scoffed. "Not a big deal?"

Scowling, Taylor glared at me. "Want to make something of it?"

I realized where his sudden anger had come from.

"No, no," I said, shaking my head. "You've got me all wrong. I'm not judging your hobby. I mean, honestly, Taylor." I gestured to my suit. "Look at me! Can you not tell I'm a fellow connoisseur of the fabric arts?"

Taylor's hackles fell. "Yeah. Guess that's true."

"Believe me, I know how much work and effort goes into quilting. Even a dragon like myself can't muster that much patience."

A slight smile appeared in the corner of Taylor's mouth. "Finally, something a dragon *can't* do."

I smiled in return, happy to see him in better spirits.

"Can I see some of your projects?" I asked.

Taylor shifted his weight from foot to foot. "I didn't bring them, but I have photos."

"I'd love to see them. Ah, they're not on your phone, are they?"

Like most reality TV contestants, Taylor had had his phone confiscated for the duration of filming. For a second, I was filled with disappointment that I wouldn't get to see his work.

But Taylor shook his head. He reached into his bag and pulled out a few printed digital photos. "Nope. When Winnie said I couldn't bring my phone, I printed these out for reference. Figured I'd need something to do at night when I was bored."

He sat on the edge of the bed and spread the photos in his hand like cards.

"Come sit next to me so you're not looking from a mile away," he offered.

My heart skipped a beat. I wasted no time slipping beside him. It wasn't just my heart that was affected by Taylor—the whole room smelled like him, and up close like this, it was impossible to ignore his scent. I tried not to think about the way it sizzled in my stomach.

"Here's a project I did for a local competition," Taylor said, handing me a photo.

It featured a huge quilt, larger than the hotel's king-size bedspread. It was made up of hundreds of smaller patches in a dizzying array of colors. Despite the patchwork, it looked cohesive and well thought out.

"Taylor," I murmured. "You made this?"

He nodded curtly. "Took a couple months of work, but I'm single and had nothing else to do, so..."

"It still blows my mind that you're single."

He shrugged. "I'm used to it. Here."

Expertly dodging the topic, he handed me another photo. This was of a smaller, softer quilt with pastel shapes. Just looking at it melted my heart.

"This was for a co-worker's newborn baby," Taylor said with undeniable warmth in his tone.

I smiled. "You like babies?"

"I love them. And not because I'm an omega," he added defensively.

"What, you think I'm some kind of alphahole who assumes all omegas are baby crazy?"

He arched a brow. "I don't know, are you?"

"Ouch, Taylor." I mimed clutching my heart.

A blush spread across his cheeks. "Sorry. I didn't mean it. You don't seem like the type... even though you're on this stupid TV show."

"So are you," I shot back.

He grinned once again like we shared an inside joke. "We're even, then."

Seeing his smile this close felt like a blessing. Taylor was absolutely gorgeous. I examined his face, burning every line of it into my memory.

"Tell me again why you're single?" I asked.

His blush deepened. A shadow fell over his face as he stared at the far wall.

"Isn't it obvious?" he muttered. "Nobody wants me."

Well, *that* was a punch to the gut.

"Excuse me?" I blurted out.

"It's true. Not my parents, not any alphas." He narrowed his eyes in pain. "All I have are my friends, and my hobby."

That explained why he seemed so close to those two, the jackal and the wolf. A fountain of sympathy opened up inside me. I touched Taylor's hand, enveloping it with my warmth.

"I don't know what their problem is," I said, unable to keep the bitterness out of my voice, "but they clearly don't know a catch when they see one."

Taylor's hand stiffened beneath mine, but he didn't jerk it away.

"Apparently, you're the only one who thinks so," he mumbled. "My parents stopped talking to me when I didn't pursue the career path they wanted."

A jolt of anger shot through me. "What?" I hissed. "What could you possibly do that offended them *that* badly?"

"University wasn't for me. Especially not business school. I didn't like the vicious competition. So I dropped out and went into a simple retail job to keep myself afloat while enjoying my hobby."

Draconic fury coursed through my veins like lava. It

took everything I had to tamp it down, otherwise I'd shift in the middle of the hotel room.

Instead, I squeezed Taylor's hand reassuringly. "Screw them."

Taylor's face was stoic, but I sensed the hurt within him. "It's fine. I'm over it."

He clearly wasn't, but held it together so he wouldn't look weak or vulnerable. How could I teach him he didn't have to be that way with me?

I blew out a long, hot sigh from my nostrils. "I'm sorry, Taylor."

"For what? You didn't do anything."

"That's not exactly true. By agreeing to be in the Dragonfate Games, I roped you into it, too. I didn't know you hated competition."

Taylor looked surprised. "No, it's not your fault, Crimson. I chose to come."

"Why, then?"

He hesitated, glancing down at the bed sheets. "I don't know."

I desperately wanted him to open up to me. No more holding back.

"We're alone, Taylor," I whispered. "You can tell me the truth."

He arched a sarcastic brow. "You're not wearing a hidden mic, are you?"

I laughed. "Strip search me, if you like."

I expected him to outright refuse, but Taylor's eyes flashed like he actually considered it. How pathetic was it for my cock to twitch because of that?

"I won't say no if you undress yourself," Taylor replied slowly.

Was that an *invitation?*

Well, shit. I couldn't refuse now—and I didn't want to.

Overflowing with excitement, I grinned as I slipped out of my blazer. Taylor's eyes tracked me as I folded it and set it neatly aside.

"No mic so far, is there?" I teased, but it was also an easy out for him in case he wanted me to stop this silly charade.

"Not yet," Taylor said, eyes flashing.

So I kept going. My silk tie and button-up shirt were next. I took my sweet time undressing, putting on a show for Taylor. I loved showing off my clothes and my body to him. I felt like the world's most expensive stripper.

Taylor's tiger eyes landed on my hip bones, now exposed. He let out a low huff of amusement. "I half expected your body hair down there to be red."

That comment sent me reeling. He was looking at me *that* closely?

"It's black, I'm afraid," I said. "Although there might be a surprise if you go even lower."

He arched a brow. "Oh?"

"Shall I resume the show?" I grinned. "Or are you satisfied that I'm not wearing a hidden mic?"

There it was—a natural end point if Taylor wanted one. Half of me expected him to take the out, since any further loss of clothing would result in a very naked dragon. But the other half of me wanted to go all the way, to bare my body *and* soul to him. It was far too late to deny it—I was smitten with this big kitten.

Taylor's sharp eyes held steady on me. Despite his practiced stoic expression, I sensed the burning cat-like curiosity inside him. Then he said the magic words: "Not yet."

A shiver rolled down my spine. My only remaining clothes were my pants and underwear.

Not wanting to disappoint Taylor, I slowly undid my

button and zipper. Then I hooked my thumbs into the waistband and shimmied out of my pants, setting them with my other things.

I was now fully naked, except for my underwear—which my half-hard cock strained against.

My skin felt hot under Taylor's intense gaze. The coolness of the hotel room air raised the hair on my arms.

"Satisfied now?" I asked huskily.

Taylor stared at my deep red briefs. "No."

I chuffed. "There's only one thing left to go. Do you really think I could hide a mic down there?"

Taylor didn't miss a beat. "You said yourself that your microphones are *very* high quality. How do I know you're not hiding some advanced technology in your underwear?"

I'd set myself up for that one.

"Well," I mused, "why don't you take a look?"

Taylor finally looked up at me. It was the first time our gazes had locked since I started undressing. An undeniable fire blazed in his eyes.

Tempted by curiosity, I looked beneath his thighs.

Oh, yes. He was definitely hard, too.

Finally, Taylor said, "Maybe I will."

I only had a second to process that before Taylor's hands landed on my hips.

As his fingers dug into me, a jolt of arousal sparked down my spine. My dragon soul roused, pounding on the walls of his cage.

"Taylor," I said in a low, thick voice.

"Hm."

How could I phrase this without sounding like a sex-crazed alpha?

"It will, ah, be difficult for me to control myself if you press onward," I said.

Taylor's palms pressed into my hip bones. He glanced up at me. "Who said I want you to control yourself?"

A wave of relief hit me. I understood now. This raw attraction was mutual.

Was that all it was, though? Simple attraction?

I didn't think so. It was too powerful, like comparing a summer drizzle to a typhoon—and what I felt towards Taylor was definitely the latter.

A pleasured growl rolled in my throat as Taylor's palm stroked across the front of my briefs. His large hands radiated warmth. My cock twitched beneath his touch, desperate after only a few seconds. Soon, I was hard enough that the fabric fought to stay in one piece.

"Pent up?" Taylor teased in that coy, calm voice I found so alluring.

"How can I help myself when a kitty is teasing me?"

Taylor snorted. "Call me a kitty again and see what happens."

My curiosity got the best of me. "What will happen, kitty?"

Taylor squeezed my sensitive cock. It was firm yet gentle, just enough to make me gasp from surprise.

"You made it sound like a threat," I said, a bit breathless.

"I can go harder." Teasing again.

I chuckled. "I give. Touch me however you like."

Taylor's palm pressed into the base of my cock and slowly moved up. That earned another groan from me. His thumb caressed the tip in a languid swirling motion, then he suddenly stopped.

"What's wrong?" I asked.

Taylor took a breath. His glassy, lust-filled eyes didn't *look* like he wanted to stop, but his willpower was strong.

"Should we be doing this?" Taylor mumbled. "Isn't the whole point of this show to find your fated mate?"

The words were on the tip of my tongue: *I've already found him.*

"Fooling around in secret won't stop the Games," I said instead.

Taylor pointedly raised a brow. "I feel like it's against the rules."

I huffed. He turned me on too much for me to care about logic. "It's a reality TV show, not a presidential race. Besides, I'm the one who initiated it by visiting you after hours. They can't exactly throw *me* off the show, can they?"

Taylor smirked. "Guess not." He dipped his thumbs into the waistband of my briefs and pulled down. "Good thing you're immune to the rules..."

I hissed as my hard cock popped out of my underwear. The cool air against my hot flesh made me shiver. Taylor examined my cock closely, like a tiger stalking his prey.

"Hey," I said. "Since when did I become nude while you're still fully dressed?"

Taylor grinned. "Since you decided to strip for my benefit."

"Ah, yes, the hidden mic. Found one yet?"

"Not yet." Taylor wrapped his fingers around the base of my cock. "I'll keep searching."

I blew out a shaky breath as Taylor gently moved up my shaft. Every movement sent electric currents tingling across my skin. My whole body felt ready to explode.

Naked and at the mercy of a teasing omega... what a vulnerable position for an alpha dragon to be in.

Taylor leaned forward, holding my gaze. His eyes flashed mischievously as his lips grazed the head of my cock. I groaned as my cock bobbed in the air, desperate for him.

What was this enchantment Taylor had cast on me? I was spellbound by him, completely at his mercy... and I loved every second of it.

Taylor's mouth engulfed me. The moan that escaped me was guttural and raw, laced with my dragon's growl. It apparently turned Taylor on too, because I felt him shudder in response.

Screw the pretense of keeping my cool.

I grabbed Taylor's shoulders, both to steady myself and to encourage him. The previously cool hotel room suddenly felt as hot and humid as a sauna as our muggy breaths and sweat mingled.

Speaking of hot, Taylor's lips on my cock were divine. The velvet heat of his mouth went straight to my balls, making them throb with need. I groaned and whined like a mewling kitten, not a ferocious dragon. This man brought me to my knees with just a calm glance and half a blowjob.

"Taylor," I growled, lacing my fingers into his thick hair.

He hummed low in reply. The vibrations shot up the length of my dick, causing me to hiss in pleasure. My cock twitched violently in Taylor's mouth, and I felt brainless with desire.

Taylor slipped off my cock with a wet pop. "What is it?"

Finding the words was nearly impossible. "You're so..."

I took too long to answer. He teased me by running his finger up the length of my sensitive shaft, which made me lose *more* brain cells.

"Say it, Crimson." He tried to sound calm, but I heard the breathy waver of his voice. He was hard, too.

I replied with the only word I could think of.

"Perfect," I murmured.

Taylor blinked, surprised. The pink on his cheeks

turned a darker color. Then he let out a scornful huff. "That's your dick talking."

"No, it's not."

Taylor didn't back down. "You're only saying that because I'm giving you head."

My chest was on fire. My dragon soul reared, protective and possessive and furious with the undeniable need to claim the omega in front of me.

"No," I snapped. "I don't exaggerate my feelings, Taylor. Even when I'm harder than a diamond."

My sudden ferocity didn't faze Taylor. He met my gaze evenly, though with less doubt than he felt before. Cautious hope shimmered in his eyes.

Suddenly, he smiled. "Good to know. It'll make me feel like less of a greedy slut when I make you come down my throat."

If I had a retort, it died the second Taylor swallowed my cock down to my balls. I let out a choked sound as Taylor deep-throated me.

My fingers curled in Taylor's hair. I groaned and bucked my hips wildly, without rhythm. The skyrocketing pleasure was too much. It built like a shaken soda bottle, then finally peaked. I came with a raw shout, seeing a pinprick galaxy of stars across my vision.

Taylor sucked me through my orgasm. His lips wrapped around my cock like it was his mission in life to get every last drop out of me. By the time my aftershocks faded, I would say he accomplished his task. Not a single bead of cum trickled down his mouth, only streaks of saliva. His hair was tousled and his cheeks were bright pink.

He looked pretty damn pleased with himself.

I stumbled forward, woozy on my knees after that

mind-shattering orgasm. Taylor caught me so I didn't fall. He helped me onto the bed next to him.

"Thanks," I said breathlessly.

He smirked. "It would be unfortunate if you bumped your head and fell into a coma during filming."

"Is that the only reason you're concerned?"

"Of course not, you dumb lizard."

My jaw dropped and I gasped loudly. "You did *not* just call me a lizard. When was the last time you saw a lizard fly and breathe fire?"

"I haven't seen *you* do either of those things," Taylor said with a wry grin. "In fact, I haven't seen this so-called dragon form of yours at all. Maybe it was all a big scam to entice contestants."

"Taylor, your audacity astounds me. I'll have you know I—"

I was interrupted by a knock on the wall, followed by a voice calling out, "Yo, Tay, you good in there? I heard moaning and screaming."

Instantly, I pursed my lips. Had I been *that* loud?

Taylor ducked his head. "Crap. Muzo heard us," he said under his breath. "You'd better go, Crimson."

My shoulders drooped in disappointment. Even if he was right, I didn't want to leave. I wanted to stay right here beside Taylor.

Pouting, I leaned against his shoulder. "But I'm so weak after coming. What if I break my knee?"

He snorted. "You won't break your knee *flying* away. Come on. I'll see you tomorrow anyway."

Stupid logic.

"Fine," I mumbled. "But what about you? You didn't get to finish."

He shrugged. "I'll deal with it myself."

That felt like such a waste. I wanted to wrap my hands around him, too. "I can quickly—"

Muzo's voice came again. "Hello, Earth to Taylor. Did you die?"

Taylor sighed, rubbing his temple. "I'm fine, Muzo. Go to bed."

"Okay..."

Once that was settled, the room fell quiet. Taylor gave me a look that indicated it was time to leave. He was right. Tomorrow was another day of the Games—another challenge, another day of filming.

Another day of me pretending I didn't already know who my final choice was.

I slowly got up from the bed. "Well... I suppose I'll see you then."

To my surprise, Taylor followed me to the balcony door. Just before I shifted, he grabbed my arm and turned me around.

He pressed a soft kiss to my cheek.

"Goodnight, Crimson," Taylor murmured. "And by the way... I never found that hidden mic."

Then he disappeared behind the hotel room curtains.

ELEVEN

Taylor

AFTER A LATE-NIGHT DEFINITELY-AGAINST-THE-RULES tryst with Crimson followed by a furious jack-off session, the last thing I wanted the following morning was a confrontation with Alaric.

I didn't get my wish.

"You *smell* like Crimson," Alaric hissed.

All the contestants had gathered in the lobby, waiting for Gaius to arrive and announce the next challenge. Upon Alaric's declaration, every single one of them turned to stare at us.

I closed my eyes and sighed. Unfortunately, that never made the problem go away.

"I don't know what you're talking about," I said as calmly as possible.

"Don't play stupid," Alaric snapped. He got right in front of me and jabbed an accusatory finger into my face. "Crimson's scent is wafting off you. Care to explain why?"

The worst part was that he was right. I'd showered in the morning, but it didn't help. Us cat shifters had keen senses of smell.

"Maybe you should get your nose checked," I said, fully

aware that I was lying, though I didn't give a shit.

Alaric's face twisted in fury. "Don't *gaslight* me."

I groaned. "Oh, come on."

Now other contestants mumbled to each other. I couldn't tell which one of us they believed, but the commotion got loud enough to grate on my nerves. The cameras ate it up, of course. This was juicy reality TV drama.

To my surprise, it was Poppy who diffused the situation. He snuck between us, soaking up the tension like a fluffy cotton ball.

"Taylor wouldn't go behind anyone's back like that," he said, gentle yet confident.

Alaric tried glaring at Poppy, but it didn't work. He was too adorable to glare at. "What do you know, wolf? Maybe *your* nose is the one that's broken!"

"My nose is fine," Poppy insisted. "All I scent on Taylor is big cat and hotel shampoo."

Wait, really? I couldn't tell if Poppy was telling the truth or making up a story for my sake. But he wouldn't do that. Maybe I'd done a better job of scrubbing Crimson's scent off my body than I assumed.

Muzo butted in, too. "Yeah, Alaric. You can't accuse Taylor of stuff without proof." He leaned closer to Alaric. "You got any? Huh?"

Alaric sneered and backed off. "Don't get so close to me, dog."

"Jackal."

"Whatever." Alaric whipped his meticulously brushed white hair and stormed off to stand on the other side of the lobby.

I blew out a sigh of relief. "Thanks, you two."

Muzo waved a hand. "Don't mention it. That guy needs to get laid. Actually, that's the point of this show, so I guess he's trying his best..."

I tried not to think about the fact that I'd been intimate with Crimson last night. It wasn't penetrative sex, but...

A shiver went down my spine when I remembered how hot Crimson looked fully nude. He was always attractive, but there was eroticism in his vulnerability. I liked it. I wanted more of it.

I bit my lip. No, I couldn't kindle those desires, not in the middle of this game show. I had to smother those feelings, otherwise our secret rendezvous would be too obvious.

But what did it mean? I could chalk it up to just a blowjob between two horny men... unless it was actually something deeper.

I swallowed the lump in my throat, wondering why that thought felt so nice.

———

AFTER HIS HOST SPIEL, Gaius led the contestants to our next challenge at the base of a craggy cliff. It was steep, but as I eyed it, I recognized it wasn't impossible to scale—for me, anyways. Cats were natural climbers, but I wasn't sure if the rest of the contestants could manage.

Would this be like the river challenge where Crimson awaited us at the top? Or was he elsewhere, watching from a distance? That only made me more determined to get there first and find out.

"All right, omegas!" Gaius announced in his usual cheerful voice. "It's day two of the Dragonfate Games! Our challenge today requires mental fortitude, physical strength, and tremendous willpower. As you can see, we're standing beneath a cliff. Your goal—" He gestured to the peak. "—is to reach the top!"

A few omegas groaned quietly. I recognized them as

the ones who struggled yesterday, but still made it out of the river. They were mostly species who had difficulty climbing. In the back of my mind, I wondered if Crimson had specifically catered these challenges towards me so I'd win, since swimming and climbing were both skills tigers excelled at.

"Once again, nothing is off limits," Gaius went on. "Climb, slither, crawl, fly, or hitch a ride—do whatever it takes to reach the top. Your reward is another chance at a date with Crimson!"

The hairs on the back of my neck rose.

I didn't *want* any of these omegas to go on a date with him.

He was mine.

The thought came on so fast and strong that it stunned me. Mine? Crimson wasn't my property. Hell, I barely knew him. Just because I'd given him a blowjob last night didn't mean anything...

That didn't dull the possessive urge gnawing at me. I wanted to win, the same as the first challenge.

But Alaric's accusation filled me with doubt. If I won again, Alaric would blow a gasket. He'd probably take his allegation to the cameras and put me on the spot. I didn't want to draw any more attention to myself.

Yet I couldn't handle the thought of Crimson choosing another omega as the winner, either. Thinking about him with someone else made me want to spit with anger.

Shit. What should I do?

"On your marks, omegas!" Gaius called out.

Everyone else beside me had shifted already. I rushed to do the same. My claws itched with impatience, but I forced myself to hold steady.

"Ready? Go!"

A dark shape blurred over my head. A bird shifter I

didn't remember from yesterday's chaos bolted upwards. An ugly feeling stewed in my stomach, but I tried remaining calm and logical. I pushed my envy aside. That was proof Crimson didn't cater the challenges towards me. Of course, a flying shifter would win over an omega who climbed.

That didn't make me feel *that* much better as the bird rocketed towards the finish line, but I focused on myself instead of my jealousy. Besides, reaching the peak first didn't automatically make him the winner of the challenge. That was up to Crimson.

I still had a chance.

By the time I leapt onto the cliffside and dug my claws into the hard earth, a few contestants were already out of the running. A horse and a deer shifter changed back to human form, shaking their heads. Their hooves and large size made it impossible to scale a sheer surface, and trying it in human form was out of the question. They'd risk breaking a bone.

Other four-legged shifters fared slightly better. Felines like me had no issue. Canines like Poppy and Muzo found purchase on earthy pockets dotting the cliffside. Their claws and smaller size helped them slowly, but surely climb up.

I paused, watching my friends. My tail swished back and forth in concern.

Muzo noticed me staring at him. "Hey, get a move on! Don't worry about us."

"Are you sure you'll be okay?" I asked.

"Positive. Right, Pops?"

Poppy was so focused on putting one shaky paw in front of the other that he didn't answer.

I was sure they'd make it eventually, so I went back to climbing. My claws and muscles made quick work of the sheer surface, although hauling my heavy weight upwards grew harder the closer I got to the top.

"You should stay down there with your *friends*."

My tail lashed at the sudden smarmy voice in my ear. Alaric was right beside me, his odd eyes narrowed in distaste. Like me, he had no issue climbing. His feline claws and long tail kept him perfectly balanced, but unlike me, he didn't have to carry an additional five hundred pounds of tiger ass.

"You'd like that, wouldn't you?" I grumbled.

"Yes. In fact, I'd love it if you dropped out of this competition."

"I bet you would. Too bad it won't happen."

We climbed and snarked at each other in tandem, evenly matched.

"I'm reaching the top," Alaric declared through his sharp teeth. "And when I do, Crimson will choose *me* as the winner."

I couldn't help the snarky laugh that came out of me. Alaric's ears flattened against his head in fury and he hissed loudly.

"What's so funny?"

"You're not Crimson's type," I said.

"Oh, and you are?" Alaric shot back venomously. "You can barely get your fat ass up this cliff!"

Okay, now he was getting on my nerves.

Baring my fangs, I growled, "You'd better watch your mouth."

Alaric smirked. "You want to slap me right off this cliff, don't you?"

That was exactly what he wanted. I knew it. His plan was to goad me until I snapped and looked bad on TV. But his plan wasn't going to work.

"I don't need to," I said, leaping a foot up the slope.

Alaric was neck-and-neck with me. He threw his lithe body upwards, then sank his claws into the earth. "And why's that?"

"Because Crimson doesn't like mean omegas like you."

Alaric looked shocked and annoyed. "I am *not* mean. I'm telling the truth."

"Whatever, Alaric."

Ignoring him, I slammed my paws into the cliff, inching up one step at a time. But my tiff with Alaric left me irritated, so I didn't pay as much attention as I should have been. My claws caught a loose rock the size of a human fist and plummeted from under my paw.

I gasped, looking down. If there was anyone beneath me, they'd get hit—and from this height, it would hurt.

My heart sank when I saw a familiar figure directly below me.

Muzo.

My body moved faster than my brain. I unlocked my claws from the cliff, twisting in midair as I fell towards him. Alaric made fun of my large size, but in this case, my weight was a blessing. I lost altitude just fast enough to outrun the plummeting rock.

I couldn't push Muzo out of the way, otherwise he'd fly off the cliff. Steeling myself, I sank my claws into the earth just above Muzo and used my body as a shield, taking the blow instead of him. I grunted as the rock hit me. It bounced off my thick haunch, then tumbled harmlessly down to the ground.

I sighed in relief. Looking down, I caught Muzo's wide eyes.

"Uh, what just happened?" he asked.

"Don't worry about it," I said.

"Well, a tiger fell out of the sky, followed by a big rock,

so it's kinda hard not to worry about it." Muzo put two and two together. "Wait, did you just save my life?"

I snorted. "Don't be so dramatic."

"I could've gotten a concussion! Or worse! You're my savior, Taylor!"

Embarrassed at his praise, I flicked my tail. "I'm leaving now."

With that misadventure over, I crept back up the cliff. Getting to the top was easy since I was fueled by leftover adrenaline. There, I joined a handful of shifters who'd already reached the finish line. Alaric was among them. He sat with his back to me, as if trying to pretend I didn't exist. That was fine with me. It was better than constantly bickering with him.

I looked around the top of the cliff. This time, Crimson was nowhere to be seen. That made me feel better, in a childish way. That meant that the bird shifter and others who'd arrived before me hadn't had some private, special moment with Crimson.

I wanted to be the only person who had those.

I heard a familiar voice huffing and puffing behind me. Muzo and Poppy had finally made it to the top together. I felt relieved to see them. Today's challenge was definitely harder than yesterday's for them. I hoped tomorrow's was easier, for their sake. As much as I wanted to win, I didn't want my friends to go home.

On the other hand, I wouldn't complain if tomorrow's challenge was difficult for a certain house cat…

"You guys okay?" I asked my friends.

Muzo shifted and gave me a weak thumbs up, while Poppy remained in his wolf form and nodded. I gave him a friendly lick between the ears before we all shifted to human form.

"Dude, I hope the cameras caught your epic moment,"

Muzo said.

He was talking about the rock again. I huffed. "It wasn't a big deal."

"It totally was! If you didn't intervene, it would've bonked me on the head like a cartoon."

A voice I didn't recognize interjected. "Yes, I was quite impressed."

I turned to see the bird from before speaking to me. Now that I caught a good look at him, I realized he was a golden eagle. I quelled the pain of jealousy I felt towards him, since he'd technically reached the top first—but that didn't mean Crimson would choose him as the winner.

"Thanks," I said. "Sorry, I didn't catch your name."

"Matteo."

"I'm Taylor."

"I know. Hard to forget the winner of the first challenge."

His tone was coy, but it lacked the venom of Alaric's jabs. Matteo seemed like a good sport, which made me feel bad for being jealous.

Gaius's announcement voice rang out. "And it looks like all of our final contestants are here! Great job today, everyone. I know it certainly wasn't easy for you four-legged folk." He winked in our direction. "Now it's time for the big moment… Who will Crimson choose as today's winner?"

As Crimson stepped out from behind Gaius, my heart skipped a beat. It hadn't been that long since I last saw him, yet it felt like an eternity. I stomped out the desire to rush over to him. What was I, a teenager with a crush?

Then I locked eyes with him. The fluttering of my heart went from a skip to a storm.

Maybe I wasn't much better than a teenager with a crush after all.

TWELVE

Crimson

_____

I WAS PERFECTLY calm as I stepped out to face the expectant crowd of omegas. There was no conflict in my mind. I already knew exactly who I'd choose as today's winner— and I hoped he knew I'd pick him, too.

The kobold crew crouched eagerly around us in a loose circle, cameras at the ready. Gaius inclined his head and offered me the mic.

"Well, Crimson? You've got a fine group of contestants here. But there can only be one winner. Who's it going to be?" Gaius prompted.

My gaze drifted naturally towards Taylor. The rest of the omegas may as well have not existed. In fact, I felt sorry that they'd been dragged into this.

Then again, before the Games began, I didn't know I'd fall for Taylor. I'd written off the whole show as frivolous, yet here I was staring at the man I wanted as my mate.

It was so quiet on the cliff, you could've heard a pin drop. The omegas, the camera crew, and Gaius all waited with bated breath for my final decision.

"For his continued display of bravery and compassion,

the omega I choose as the winner of today's challenge is Taylor."

Taylor's eyes flashed, but he expertly kept his composure. The same couldn't be said for some of the other contestants. That white-haired omega, Alaric, was visibly furious. I half expected him to leap at Taylor and attempt to throw him off the edge of the cliff. Not that I'd let that happen. Meanwhile, Taylor's friends looked happy for him, congratulating him earnestly. Their friendship warmed my heart.

I'd watched the whole challenge from behind the scenes. Honestly, I nearly had a heart attack when Taylor launched himself off the cliff in order to protect Muzo. But I understood why he did it. Taylor's stoic exterior hid a kind, caring personality. It was one more thing I loved about him.

Love… Yes, I was certain about the feeling now. It couldn't be anything else.

Gaius took control of the situation. He sauntered over to Taylor, thrusting the mic at him. "And for the second challenge, Taylor is our winner! How do you feel about that?"

Taylor shifted his weight uncomfortably. He clearly didn't enjoy being in the spotlight. "Fine, I suppose."

Gaius laughed heartily. "He wins twice in a row, and he feels fine about it!"

There were sour expressions among some of the other contestants. I would've felt bad about consistently letting them down, but in the end, the Dragonfate Games were about my brothers and me finding our mates. I couldn't help it that Taylor drove me wild.

"Now let's reveal what Taylor has won this time," Gauis began with a mischievous grin. "You've got another date tonight with the alpha dragon himself, but this is no ordinary dinner date. There's a twist." He winked at the nearest camera. "What will it be? Stay tuned."

ANNOYINGLY, the crew did a damn good job of keeping me in the dark. I wasn't allowed to know the "twist" of my date with Taylor. Judging by the challenges thus far, I wouldn't be surprised if they threw us out of a helicopter together or something similarly stupid.

The date was set on the beach in the evening again. This time, there was no platform or pop-up restaurant. As far as I could tell, it was just us, the sand, and the sea. So far, I couldn't complain.

I wore a striking white suit tonight with my signature red tie to match the streak in my hair. There was no doubt, I was the most well-dressed man on this island.

But when Taylor appeared, he took my breath away. Even in his simple black T-shirt and jeans, I wanted to ravish him. Hell, he could wear a potato sack and still make my cock twitch.

"Good evening, Taylor," I said, smiling.

He nodded politely. "Hey, Crimson."

While I made no attempt to hide my affection towards him, Taylor seemed hesitant to do the same. Did the cameras make him shy? Or was he holding back his feelings for me?

From the corner of my eye, I noticed Gaius examining us. For all his boisterous showmanship, he had a keen eye. I wondered if he suspected something going on between us behind the scenes. But if he did, he didn't comment. He strolled up to us with a beaming smile.

"Here we are for the second date! Crimson, Taylor, are you two ready?" he asked.

"As ready as we can be to face the unknown," I said dryly.

That earned a small snort of laughter from Taylor.

Gaius chuckled. "Come on, where's your sense of adventure? After all, we didn't plan all *this* for nothing..."

As he finished speaking, a pair of kobolds wheeled out a gleaming gold post. Attached to it were matching pairs of gold handcuffs.

One pair for me and one for Taylor, I realized.

Whichever one of my brothers thought of this ridiculous concept was going to pay...

Gaius clapped his hands together. "What do we have here? Why, it's a game of Look, But Don't Touch! What does that mean for our pair? The two of them will be handcuffed to this pole for a whole hour. In that time, they can do anything they wish—except touch each other. But if these two are truly fated, is that even possible? It's going to be an epic battle of restraint and willpower!"

Taylor stared deadpan at Gaius. I, too, was ready to throttle him.

Unfortunately, Gaius was immune to our death glares. "Take your places, if you please," he prompted us cheerfully.

Taylor shot me a silent, pleading look. I didn't want to submit to this idiotic charade either, but if it was part of the show, I couldn't refuse. I sighed and offered my wrists for Gaius to cuff me to the gilded post. In response, Taylor swallowed a groan and did the same. At least if we were forced to act out some bullshit, we were in it together.

The chains on the handcuffs weren't very long. There was less than a foot of leeway between our cuffed wrists and the gilded post between us. If I was here with any other person, this would have been a deeply uncomfortable situation. But it was Taylor. I could've stood here and stared at him forever, which I realized was the whole point of this stupid game.

Gaius beamed when the staff finished setting us up together. "Here they are, the alpha and omega who've been on not one, but two dates now," he explained to the camera. "In this game of Look, But Don't Touch, their willpower will be put to the ultimate test. Can these two really spend an entire hour in close proximity without breaking? Let's find out. The timer starts… Now!"

Taylor rolled his eyes. "This is ridiculous," he mumbled.

"I agree."

"I mean, honestly, who comes up with this stuff?"

I tilted my head. "I can easily think of a few people…"

I imagined Aurum and Saffron cackling as they cooked up this idea and pitched it to Duke.

Taylor sighed. "An hour isn't too long. At least our mouths aren't duct-taped closed."

I chuckled. "Don't give them any ideas."

That earned an amused twitch of Taylor's lips. "You're right. I'll keep any forms of strange and unusual punishment to myself."

"Punishment?" I grinned. "You hate spending time with me that much?"

"If it involves being handcuffed to post for an hour, then I'm leaning towards yes."

I let out a pained noise. "Taylor, all you do is wound me."

"You can take it, alpha dragon," Taylor replied, putting a snarky emphasis on the last two words. That was another thing I liked about him. Since we were so rare, the whole alpha dragon concept was plastered all over the show as a marketing tactic. Many of the contestants bought into it, too. Frankly, it made my skin crawl when Alaric flirted with me during the meet and greet, fawning all over the fact that I was an alpha dragon. It was *what* I was, not *who* I was. Taylor was the only omega who saw that.

"So…" Taylor looked around. The camera crew was a good distance away to give us space, though their excellent lenses were likely capturing close-up shots as we spoke. "How would you like to spend this next hour, Crimson?"

The way he said my name sent a chill down my spine. "I can certainly think of a few ways."

A brief flicker of pink appeared on Taylor's cheeks before he huffed and brought himself back to earth. "I see you weren't listening earlier, lizard brain."

He leaned in closer so his forehead nearly brushed mine. "Hey, that offends me."

"The name of the game is Look, But Don't Touch, remember?"

To be fair, he was right, I hadn't been paying attention at all. My brain was occupied with the fact that I was handcuffed together with my future mate. Maybe lizard brain wasn't too far off.

I scoffed. "What, so I'm not allowed to do this?"

I raised my cuffed wrists and reached out a finger to touch Taylor's hand.

Out of nowhere, Gaius karate chopped me away.

"Ow!" I cried. "Where the hell did you come from?"

Gaius tutted at me, wagging a finger like I was a child. "Ah, ah! Looks like Crimson didn't understand the rules."

"What rules? You never mentioned any."

"Taylor just explained them, but allow me to elaborate. You may look at Taylor, but you cannot touch him for the duration of one hour. No holding hands, no hugging, no kissing on the cheek—or kissing elsewhere…" He winked.

"I'm going to turn you into chicken nuggets," I grumbled.

Gaius tapped my handcuffs. "You're free to do so after your hour's up. Until then, good luck staying apart from your date." He arched a brow dramatically. "That is, unless the two of you aren't fated mates after all."

That random remark turned my stomach. What was that supposed to mean?

Before I could interrogate him, Gaius strolled back to the safety of the camera crew. A burning anger roiled in my gut. How dare he insinuate that?

"Crimson?" Taylor asked quietly, "are you all right?"

The sound of his voice calmed me down. Slightly. Turning back towards him, I sighed through my nostrils. "I'm fine. Just thinking about plucking all of Gaius's feathers."

"Because of what he said?" When I nodded stiffly, Taylor said, "don't worry about it. He was only trying to stir drama and rile you up." He smirked. "And it worked."

I flushed, feeling a bit embarrassed. "I apologize. I'm normally in better control of my temper."

"You don't have to be. I like seeing different sides of you."

"You do?" I asked, my brows shooting up in surprise.

Taylor shrugged. "What's the point in only knowing one facet of you? That's not what dating is about. I'm supposed to know the real you, aren't I?" He glanced down at the sand. "But what do I know? It's not like I'm a master of dating."

Dammit. I wanted to hold his hands, to reassure him physically. But I couldn't because of this farce.

"I don't care how much dating experience you have," I said. "That was exactly what I needed to hear, Taylor. Thank you."

He blushed again. This time, it didn't immediately disappear off his face.

I edged closer to him, almost as much as the chains would allow. When I reached the end of them, I was practically on top of the gilded pole separating us. I cursed the damn thing. I wished I was on top of Taylor instead.

From this distance, the scent of him flooded my nose. A shiver went down my spine. He was absolutely delectable. I wanted to bury my face in his neck, his chest, even his armpits… I wanted to taste the salt of his skin on my tongue, to run my fingers through his hair and across his body.

Taylor's scent flicked a switch in my mind. My instincts flared up. My cock twitched in my pants.

I exhaled shakily, trying to calm myself down. This was being filmed. I had to remember that. I couldn't look like a lust-crazed dragon on TV… Unless that was exactly what the producers wanted. Wasn't that the point of this silly game?

I met Taylor's gaze. He seemed to notice the change in me. There was a glassy film over his eyes, similar to what I saw last night during our secret meeting.

"Holding up?" Taylor asked. That was code for, *can you keep it in your pants?*

"Well enough," I replied. "What about you?"

"I'm fine."

But I knew well enough that he wasn't fine. I heard the stiffness in his voice. It wasn't something the audience or anyone else would pick up on. Nobody except me.

Upon closer inspection, I noticed Taylor had inched closer to me, too. His legs nearly brushed up against the pole.

I wished I could replace the damn thing with *my* pole…

The thought sent another tingle of arousal through my body. I clenched my eyes shut and breathed.

Seriously, Crimson? Getting horny on TV?

This wasn't like me at all. I was calm. Collected.

Taylor did something to me. I felt deranged over him.

Being this close to him while touching was barred was absolutely torturous. I'd rather have my claws clipped off one by one.

A draconic growl built in my throat. My dragon soul stirred, pacing restlessly. It wanted to burst free and claim what was mine.

And Taylor *was* mine.

Taylor cleared his throat, wrenching me back to reality. "So. Collected any new suits lately?"

The mention of my hoard perked me up. I met his gaze, blinking away the haze of arousal.

Taylor understood what was happening to me. He'd seen my horny side last night. He must've recognized what was happening right now, and he knew me well enough to distract me from getting worse.

"The last one was… about a month ago," I said.

"What color was it?"

"Deep navy, almost black in certain lighting."

"Sounds nice. I'd like to see it," Taylor said with a smile that melted me.

"I'll show it to you sometime," I promised. "As long as you show me more of your quilts."

Taylor's eyes widened. A gentle, honest look came over his expression. Just like he'd appealed to my passion, I appealed to his. I wanted him to know that I remembered every single thing he told me, and I always would.

Taylor's smile deepened. "Sure. But trust me, you'll get bored if you let me blather on."

A good-natured possessive growl reverberated in my throat. "Never."

He looked even more surprised. Had no one ever bothered to share his interests before? Apparently not, given Taylor's previous statement about his lack of dates.

I didn't mind. In fact, that pleased me. Taylor was mine. Nobody else's. The thought of some other alpha's hands on him infuriated me. I wouldn't feel fully satisfied until I'd claimed him, proving my love for him.

I licked my lips. He was so close, yet I couldn't touch him. Why hadn't I touched him more last night? I'd let him take control. He'd given me the best blowjob of my life, and it killed me that I couldn't return the favor right here and now. They'd definitely have to cut *that* out on the editing room floor...

As I slipped back into horny-thoughts territory, Gaius's voice rang out.

"And... time! Wow, our two contestants managed to stay apart for sixty whole minutes. Honestly, I'm surprised. For a few seconds there, it looked like these two lovebirds were about to go at it!" Gaius shook his head and shot me a knowing look. "Either they have the strongest willpower known to man, or maybe... they're not fated after all."

I felt the sting of whiplash. My gaze snapped towards Gaius. Anger coursed through my veins, and my skin prickled with fury.

"Crimson?" Taylor asked. "Are you okay?"

His voice sounded like it came from a different room. I barely heard him over the roaring blood in my ears.

Gaius definitely noticed the change in my demeanor, but he locked eyes with me and kept going anyway. "Our game of Look, But Don't Touch went nowhere. Will future dates with Taylor and Crimson end the same way?" He paused, letting the tension hang off his last words. "Or will Crimson choose a different omega next time?"

My patience, hanging by a thread, snapped.

And so did the chains binding me.

The shift came over me fast and hard. In the blink of an eye, my body exploded in size. Massive leathery wings jutted out of my back, and a row of spikes flowed down my spine. My mouth twisted into a fanged maw, and my fingers became sharp claws.

As I fell forward, my long, powerful tail helped keep my balance. But that didn't stop me from landing right on top of Taylor.

The tip of my snout pressed against his nose. I breathed hard. In my dragon form, his scent was even sweeter, even more delicious. I sucked it in like a drug.

I wanted nothing more than to ravage him right here, now. I didn't care if we were surrounded by people, or that we were on camera. My alpha dragon instincts reared up in full force, roaring the word *mate* over and over in my skull. I wanted to bury myself inside Taylor and breed him.

A soft touch on the side of my scaly maw jerked me back to reality. Taylor lay beneath me, flat and prone against the sand. He made no effort to get up or push me away. He seemed content lying there. Despite being pinned to the ground by a huge dragon, there wasn't even a single flash of fear in his eyes.

My heart sizzled with affection for him. I slowly closed my eyes as Taylor stroked my face. His touch was both calming and erotic. I didn't feel as angry as I had a few seconds ago, but now I was horny again. I wished I could flap my wings and blow all the cameras away.

Fortunately, I had *just* enough presence of mind not to do that. Duke would be pissed at me.

"It's okay, Crimson," Taylor murmured.

I shivered at the way he said my name.

"There's no need to be upset," he said. "I'm here. I'm not going anywhere."

I blew out a hot, shaky breath from my nostrils. The

force of it ruffled Taylor's hair. Then I felt a gradual change in my body. My majestic, powerful dragon shrank back inside of me until I straddled Taylor in my human form.

The beach was dead silent. For once, even Gaius didn't have anything to say.

The cameras still rolled. The look on Duke's face told me everything I needed to know. They'd just struck TV gold.

Taylor had tamed the dragon.

THIRTEEN

Taylor

LAST NIGHT when Crimson appeared on my balcony, it felt like a dream.

Tonight, my heart hammered with anticipation, like I was standing on the edge of the cliff again. Expectant. Anxious. Waiting for something to happen.

When I heard the familiar thud of his weight landing on the balcony, my nerves floated away.

He'd come again.

I threw the sliding door open. Crimson didn't greet me. He rushed inside with a crazed look in his eyes and grabbed my shoulders.

"Taylor," he breathed.

"I know."

His pupils narrowed into slits, reminding me of his draconic nature. A thrill jolted through me.

"You do something to me," he muttered.

I smirked. "I know," I repeated. I hesitated for a moment, then said, "You do something to me, too."

Crimson licked his lips. His voice was thick and husky. "Like what?"

"Like…" I huffed, shaking my head. "Like making me want to quit this stupid game and leave this island."

In the next second, Crimson slammed me against the wall. His fingers dug into me like claws. His eyes were wide and burned like embers.

Before he could say anything, I chuckled.

"What?" he growled.

I sneaked my arms around his waist, pulling him closer. "You really fell for that?"

"Fell for what?"

"I was teasing you, lizard brain." I angled my face towards his. I practically felt the phantom sensation of my tiger whiskers brushing against his skin. "I wanted to see your reaction."

Crimson slowly blinked in understanding. Then he glared at me. "You are *so* mean."

"You're the one who just pinned me to the wall," I reminded him wryly.

"Because the thought of you leaving nearly made me shift and destroy this whole building," he muttered.

I smiled as my fingers slipped beneath his blazer, roaming the small of his back. "You have a bit of a temper, don't you?"

"It's a dragon thing. When our mates threaten to disappear, we get… fiery."

My heart stumbled over itself. "Your mate?"

Crimson's expression was dead serious. "Yes."

I forgot how to breathe for a second. I'd given him a blowjob, and sure, I caught feelings for him…

But Crimson just called me his mate. The connotations of that were much deeper. I'd given up the fantasy of ever being an alpha's mate. For my entire adult life, nobody wanted me.

Crimson must've seen the shadow of doubt flicker

across my face. A feral growl rumbled in his throat. He pressed his chest against mine.

"Don't," he warned softly.

"What?" I shot back.

"I see you thinking too hard." He tilted his face. His lips were an inch from mine. "Don't think, Taylor. Just feel."

He pushed his hips forward. Our already hard cocks brushed together.

I sucked in a sharp breath at the sudden jolt of pleasure. That was the first time he'd reciprocated my touch. I didn't expect anything in return, but...

"You're doing it again," Crimson growled.

As he spoke, he aggressively shoved his palm against the bulge of my pants. "Stop thinking."

I gasped. The warmth pooling in the pit of my stomach felt so good. I couldn't help the soft moan that escaped from my lips.

Crimson grinned, pleased by the sound. He didn't hold back, either. I saw the glint of his sharp teeth. His dragon side slipped out.

As Crimson palmed my erection, I felt my doubts fading away. But there was one thing I needed to know before I let loose.

"Why did you shift earlier?" I asked between breaths.

Crimson paused stroking me for a second, then resumed. "Because of my asshole friend, Gaius." He sounded annoyed. "He knows I'm crazy for you, so he goaded me on purpose by implying we weren't fated mates."

Butterflies fluttered in my chest. "You're crazy for me?"

"Is that not obvious?"

I was speechless. A hot blush spread across my cheeks. Every part of me was burning up.

"I… I didn't know," I admitted weakly.

An adorable sound reverberated in Crimson's throat, halfway between a rolling purr and a growl. "Then I'll make it obvious for you."

He flicked his thumb across the tip of my aching cock. I cried out loudly, then bit my lip so I wouldn't wake up the whole hotel.

Crimson hissed. His mouth edged closer, hovering just above mine. "Don't hold back. Let me hear you."

That was his horny brain talking. "If anyone finds out you're here, I could be kicked off the show," I reminded him.

Crimson made a sour face, like a kid who couldn't have a cookie before dinner. "Fine." He dug the heel of his palm into my throbbing cock.

"But when this Drake-forsaken show is finally over, I'd better hear you make every noise in the damn book."

That sent a shiver down my spine. "Is that a threat, alpha?" I teased.

He got so close, I could taste his breath. "It's a promise."

I bit back a groan as he touched me. My ability to think hung by a thread. As my doubts melted away, all I felt was the pleasure Crimson gave me, along with the fierce possessiveness radiating from him. When he spontaneously shifted into his dragon form earlier, I wasn't afraid. Startled, at most. As his massive, scaly weight hovered over me, I felt safe. Wanted. *Needed*.

Nobody else ever made me feel that way.

The tension evaporated from my muscles. I submitted to Crimson's hold. He stepped up instantly. He didn't allow me to fall. He pressed me to the wall, supporting my weight with his strong arms.

I was so used to standing on my own two feet that it felt

odd for someone else to carry me. But Crimson was there. Crimson would catch me.

For the first time in my life, it felt safe to let go.

"You weren't afraid when I shifted," Crimson murmured in my ear.

"No." A beat passed. "You were sexy."

He laughed. "That's just the response I wanted."

"Did you want to fuck me on that beach?" I asked.

Crimson's teeth grazed the shell of my ear. "Of course."

I shuddered for multiple reasons. "Would you have, if nobody was watching?"

"Taylor, I barely held back from breeding you while the cameras were rolling."

I groaned. That was so fucking hot. My cock twitched violently against Crimson's palm. I craved his raw touch without my pants in the way.

"Crimson," I breathed.

He hummed in reply, since he was busy licking a wet line down my neck.

"Is Gaius wrong?" I asked.

"He's wrong about plenty of things," Crimson said dryly. "You'll have to be more specific."

I let out an amused huff. "That you should date someone else."

Crimson paused at the nook where my neck met my shoulder.

Then he bit me.

An electric burst of pain and pleasure exploded in my blood. I moaned, tossing my head back against the wall, then clamped my mouth shut so I wouldn't yell. I felt his dragon fangs sink into my skin, but the pain was brief, like being injected with a needle. As he sucked the wound, pleasure bloomed in its wake. My cock throbbed harder.

When Crimson pulled away, he licked his lips. "I just claimed you. Does that answer your question?"

I glanced down at where he'd bit me. A row of dragon fang marks remained, along with a blossoming bruise.

"Oh, good," I said. "Now I've got to wear a turtleneck I don't own to hide this hickey."

Crimson smirked. "Oops."

"What happened to hiding our trysts?"

"Couldn't help myself. Wear a scarf or something." Crimson leaned in, his ruby eyes blazing. "Because I'm going to cover you in these. I need you to know that you're mine."

And then he kissed me.

My gasp was swallowed up as Crimson crushed our lips together. His tongue shoved into my mouth, dominating me. I shut my eyes and threw away the last of my dignity. It felt too good to hold back anymore. I moaned as Crimson claimed my mouth, then finally pulled away to let me breathe. A wild, predatory look flashed in his eyes. I found that I loved being at the mercy of this dragon.

My dragon.

But Crimson wasn't the only one doing the touching. I'd untucked his white shirt and sneaked my hands against his bare back. It felt illicit to touch his soft, smooth skin beneath his clothes, even though I saw him fully naked last night.

"You're so—" Crimson gently bit my lower lip. "Fucking irresistible."

Pleasure rolled through me. The kissing and touching twisted in a velvety knot below my stomach, making me weak in the knees.

I wasn't used to letting go like this. I wasn't used to willingly submitting. And I definitely wasn't used to being smothered in affection by the hottest man ever...

But for Crimson, I was glad to make an exception.

His palm caressed my cock in languid circles, squeezing whimpers from my lips. The sounds that escaped me were shameful... Even when I jerked off in private, I kept it quiet, never allowing myself to fully bask in the pleasure. Crimson demanded it of me now. He wanted honesty and vulnerability. He manipulated my body in just the right ways. It was like he knew exactly which magic buttons to press to make me react.

Crimson let out a primal growl in between kisses. "You're mine."

The low throb on my shoulder reminded me of that. I shivered in a pleasant way.

"Do you know that?" Crimson asked, his voice low and ragged. In these hazes of lust, he was different from the calm, collected man he portrayed himself as for the public. I saw the hidden side of him—the draconic side. The one who bared his fangs and clutched possessively at his desires.

And right now, *I* was his desire.

For some reason, I hesitated to answer him. He kept saying it, and I *wanted* to believe it...

Crimson paused. He stared at me sharply. "Taylor."

"What?"

"Tell me you know."

I met his gaze. "What does it mean to be yours, Crimson?"

He blinked slowly, like the question never occurred to him. A gentleness appeared on his face. He kissed the corner of my mouth softly.

"I forgot you've never been with a dragon," he admitted with a grin. "Which is good. Because I would've torn him limb from limb."

"Thank you for mauling my hypothetical dragon ex."

He laughed, then leaned closer so our foreheads touched. Warmth and affection radiated from him like a furnace. I found myself relaxing in its glow.

"When you belong to an alpha dragon, you are their world," Crimson said. There was no hint of exaggeration in his tone. "That dragon will do *anything* for you. They would set their precious hoard on fire if you asked it."

My eyes widened. I'd heard tales of how possessive dragons were over their hoards, but I didn't know how much they reflected reality.

Crimson grinned. "For context, I nearly bit off my brother Jade's head the other day for stepping into my hoard space without asking. So you *know* that's a big deal."

"Ah. Glad you didn't behead him."

Crimson's hand left my cock, giving it a break from the relentless pleasure. Then his palms roamed down my sides, leaving tingles in their wake.

"I already told you I wasn't a fan of the Dragonfate Games," Crimson said. "But beyond the whole reality TV farce, I couldn't deny it had a purpose."

"To find a mate?" I offered.

He smirked. "You make it sound so easy."

"No. I know it's not."

"But it's even harder for us dragons." Crimson glanced out the window. The beach was dark and still. The moonlight reflected off the slow waves bumping against the shore. "Me and my brothers... our lives are here on this island. There are no other shifters. We only have each other. As you can imagine, that doesn't make for a very exciting dating scene." He grinned.

"Why not go out into the world?" I asked.

Crimson scoffed. "To live among humans? No, thank you."

"It's not *that* bad once you get used to it." But even as I said it, I knew I didn't sound convincing.

Crimson shook his head. "No offspring of mine—full dragon or half-dragon—will be forced to hide their true identity."

I stared at the floor. He wasn't wrong. If he lived among humans like I did, his offspring couldn't be truly authentic. They'd be forced to hide their beast side like I did. And worse, humans didn't believe dragons were real. If they *did* see one, how would they react?

"There are other communities," I suggested. "Ones made of only shifters. You could look there."

Crimson snorted. "You mean the ones made up of their own kind, who shun any species not their own?"

I grimaced. "Yeah. Those."

Shifter-only communities were few and far between, and like Crimson derisively pointed out, they usually weren't welcoming of outsiders. They were so afraid of the outside world that they only accepted their own shifter species.

"The world is a big place. I'm sure there must be groups of mixed shifters," I pointed out.

"Maybe so," Crimson admitted. "But this is my home, Taylor. This is where my family is. I want my offspring to be raised among their uncles in this beautiful land."

I'd deliberately moved away from my family after they stopped talking to me, but Crimson was on good terms with his. It made sense for him to want to stay here.

He tilted my chin up and warmly met my gaze. "Taylor. I want *you* to be part of my family."

My heart twisted. The kissing and touching were incredible—but this soulful declaration hit me deeper than any of that. It took my breath away. I stared at Crimson in disbelief, wondering if I'd hit my head on that cliff and fallen into a realistic dream.

"That's what it means to be mine," Crimson whispered close to my face. The sensation of his breath against my lips made me shiver. "I want you to be *my* omega. My mate. I want to worship you daily. I want to fulfill your every whim, every desire." His dragon's growl slipped into his voice again, making his chest rumble as he pressed against me. "Do you know how much it pained me to be apart from you last night?"

I'd thought the discomfort was mine alone. "Yes," I said honestly. "I felt it, too. That nagging feeling that you should've stayed."

Crimson's eyes flashed like rubies. "This all happened for a reason, Taylor. Fate brought us together."

"I thought it was my stupid friend and your dumb brothers," I teased, wrapping my arms around his neck.

He grinned and leaned into it. "That too. But fate was the driving force. That's what I believe."

My chest felt airy, my knees weak. I'd never allowed myself to believe in fated mates before... but I'd also never opened up to anybody the way I did with Crimson. The way he looked at me couldn't be faked. It was pure, raw, primal love.

A dragon's love.

As he held me, I angled my hips forward. My cock brushed against his again.

"So, when you mentioned offspring," I began. "Whose, exactly, did you mean?"

He huffed and glared at me. "Come on, Taylor. I didn't go on my whole possessive spiel for you to miss the point."

I smirked. "I didn't miss the point. Did it occur to you that maybe I just want to hear you say it out loud?"

A sound like a reptilian purr vibrated in his throat.

"In that case..." He leaned in to speak in my ear. "It's you. Only you. And if I can't have you, I want nobody else. I want to *breed* you, Taylor. I'm going to fill you to the brim. Impregnate you."

I shivered, both at his words and the feeling of his breath against my sensitive skin.

Crimson ran his hand over my stomach. "I want to see you swollen with my egg. Maybe a whole clutch."

I let out an amused snort. "Let's not get greedy."

Crimson pouted. "But you'd be so cute with a bigger tummy."

"How big is a dragon egg, anyway? And how do you know it'd be an egg at all?"

Crimson held out his hands in front of his chest. "About this big. And dragon genes are strong. I'm sure it's going to be an egg."

His absolute confidence about knocking me up was an unexpected turn-on. I grabbed his hands and put them on my ass so he'd pull me closer.

"Put an egg in me, then," I whispered.

A barely perceptible shift happened in Crimson's blazing eyes. His draconic facet took over. With a possessive growl, Crimson grabbed me and pinned me to the bed.

I wasn't a small omega—I was nearly as big as Crimson—so his power and speed surprised me. Hell, getting pinned down aroused me more than I expected. It thrilled me that behind Crimson's well-dressed and graceful exterior was a ferocious dragon. One who'd bit me, and claimed me for all time.

One who was about to put a baby in me.

On top of me, Crimson breathed hard, like he held back by a thread. "Unless you want me to rip them with my teeth," he muttered, "I suggest you take your clothes off."

I discarded my clothes before Crimson destroyed them. The next second, Crimson launched at my neck, kissing and nipping down to my collarbone. I whimpered at the mingling pain and pleasure. Then Crimson brushed his thumbs across my nipples and I gasped. That felt unexpectedly good.

Crimson smirked, pleased at my reaction. His eyes raked over my naked body. It was slow and meaningful, like he was seeing a work of art for the first time. I blushed under his scrutiny.

"What?" I mumbled.

Crimson didn't reply. He ran his hands down my chest, curving his fingers over the contours of my form. When he reached my hip bones, he made a possessive purr-growl sound.

"Mine," he mumbled.

His hands swept lower. He carefully circled around the base of my swelling cock. Fucking tease.

I thought that was his destination, but Crimson went lower. He bowed his head to kiss my thighs, running kisses all the way to my ankle. That made me flustered. He didn't just pin me to the bed to fuck me—he meant to be truly intimate.

"You're gorgeous, Taylor," he said, drawing up. "Every inch of you."

I didn't know what to say, so I stared at him, blushing hard.

Crimson chuckled. "You're bad at taking compliments." Before I could snark back, he added, "So I'll have to shower you in them."

"You don't have to—"

"Your cock is *huge*," Crimson said. He lay across my lap, pawing my erection with a mischievous look.

"Oh, you meant *that* kind of compliment."

"I can give other kinds," he said coyly. "Like... your wet hole is so filthy-hot."

A violent shudder ran down my spine. The dirty talk went straight to my balls.

Desperate for him to touch me, I writhed beneath him. "Don't tease," I grumbled.

With an impish grin, Crimson slipped two fingers against the rim of my entrance. "Who's teasing?"

I swallowed a choked sound. He barely touched me, but it felt so good. A flush of heat flew through my body. I craved more.

"Your hole is twitching," Crimson remarked. "How cute."

"Put them in me."

With a smug look, Crimson eased one finger past the ring of muscle. I hissed in relief. I'd felt so empty when he teased me. I *needed* to be filled.

"Another," I demanded.

"Wow, greedy," Crimson said playfully. I thought I saw the flash of his dragon fangs as he slid a second finger in to join the first. The stretching sensation sent a jolt along my skin. It was good, but it still wasn't enough.

My tiger's growl entered my voice. "That won't cut it."

Crimson looked surprised, then laughed. "Is that right, kitty?"

I made a grumpy face at him. But my disapproval at the nickname was forgotten when Crimson withdrew his fingers and hiked my legs up over his shoulders. An anticipatory thrill shot through me. My needy hole twitched. I felt my leaking omega slick trickling down my ass.

Crimson saw it, too. His eyes widened and he licked his lips. "You're that excited?"

"Obviously," I grumbled.

With a throaty grunt, Crimson freed his cock. It was hard and long, the head gleaming with a bead of pre-cum.

Something came over me. I fully succumbed to my lust. I wanted him in me *now*.

"Fuck me, Crimson," I growled.

For a second, Crimson's eyes glowed red. Then he snatched my hips, aligned the head of his cock with my entrance, and entered me.

I threw my head back against the pillow and hissed through my teeth. It wasn't painful, but Crimson's cock stretched me wider than his fingers had.

But gods, it felt amazing to be full. It scratched an itch I didn't know I had.

"How do you feel?" Crimson asked, his voice hoarse with arousal.

"Good. Keep going."

Sweat dripped down my brow as Crimson's cock filled me. I didn't hold back my moans. My skin felt hot and sensitive, prickling with electricity. As I focused on my breathing, Crimson's scent filled my nose. The spicy alpha musk combined with his naturally alluring smell made me dizzy. I could've laid there forever.

Crimson picked up the pace, panting hard. His breathing was ragged and uneven. His slow movements turned into deep, body-rocking thrusts. I groaned with pleasure each time his cock bottomed out inside me. When I gripped the headboard behind me, I felt my tiger claws jut out and dig into the wood, but I couldn't stop the mini-shift from happening. The way Crimson fucked me was raw and animalistic. I liked it. If it was less intense, it wouldn't be quite as satisfying.

Or maybe it would. Maybe any sex with Crimson would be just as enjoyable. There was only one way to find out.

The rising pleasure built within me until I couldn't think. Just like Crimson said, I could only *feel*.

And what I felt when I watched him fucking me...

It was something deeper than lust.

"Crimson," I said hoarsely.

Without pausing, he met my gaze.

"Kiss me."

He didn't waste a second. With his cock still plowing into me, he leaned over and captured my lips in a hungry, passionate, breathless kiss. I moaned into him. Our tongues twisted together in the velvety wetness of each other's mouths.

The burst of arousal made my balls throb. My hand flew down to my cock and I jerked myself off as we kissed. I couldn't think of anything except how good this felt—and how much I loved Crimson.

Yeah, that was it.

This feeling *was* love, wasn't it?

"Crimson," I moaned against his lips.

An affectionate, draconic growl escaped him. "I'm listening."

"I..."

I wanted to say it. I wanted him to know how I really felt. But it seemed like such a monumental confession. Was it overly sentimental to say it during sex? Would Crimson think it was silly?

"Taylor."

Crimson's burning gaze locked on mine. His eyes sparkled. They looked so *alive*, like embers danced in his irises.

"I love you," Crimson stated.

Time slowed. I forgot how to breathe.

Crimson kissed me, gentle and soft.

"I love you," he murmured. "*Only* you. Don't ever forget that." A smirk curved his lips. "And if you do, let me know so I can remind you. Like *this*."

Crimson pressed his lips to mine—at the same time, he thrust deeper into me.

The building pressure of emotion and sensation hit their peak. I came with a moan that culminated in a roar. My muscles clamped down on Crimson's cock. He hissed, burying his face in my neck as his orgasm hit. He flooded my depths with his seed. I felt its sticky wetness coating my insides, making me even more deliciously full.

As the euphoria faded, I noticed a dull pain in my neck. When I glanced down, I noticed Crimson looking sheepish—along with a new bruise next to the first.

"Sorry," he mumbled. "I bit you again..."

I snorted. "Couldn't help yourself, could you, lizard brain?"

He sighed and rested his cheek on my shoulder. "I deserve that."

I grinned, putting my arm around him. "It's fine. I don't mind the love bites. But next time, I'll bite you back."

Crimson snuggled into my neck. "I look forward to it."

FOURTEEN

Crimson
_____

I DREAMED that all six of my brothers flew above my bed in their dragon forms, incessantly and very rudely dropping boulders on me. The boulders got bigger and bigger, making a huge racket as they bounced off my head like ping pong balls.

Then, as I grumpily awakened, I realized it wasn't boulders making all that noise.

Someone was banging on the door.

And *then* I remembered, I was definitely not supposed to be naked in Taylor's bed.

Early dawn light filtered through the windows. Cursing, I roused Taylor, who was still fast asleep. I didn't think he was the type to sleep through such a racket. The sex we had last night really must've knocked him out.

"I hate construction in the morning," Taylor grumbled, still half asleep.

"It's not construction," I whispered loudly. "You've got an angry neighbor."

"Wha...?"

Taylor blearily opened his eyes and sat up. His eyes

flashed with warmth when he saw me, but the banging on the door quickly drew his attention.

"Who the hell is that?" Taylor asked, reaching over the side of the bed for his discarded shirt.

A furious, shrill voice called out, "You'd better open this damned door, tiger!"

"Ah," I said simply.

Taylor made a face like he'd rather get a root canal than deal with Alaric right now. Huffing irritably, he put on his underwear and stood up. He didn't bother getting fully dressed, which said a lot about his patience with the house cat.

"Should I talk to him?" I offered.

Taylor raised a brow. "That's the worst thing you could do." He sighed. "I can handle him. You'd better go."

Pain stung me, but it wasn't as bad as last time. Now I knew Taylor's true feelings, and he knew mine. Affection swirled in my chest.

"All right," I relented. "Don't let him rip your pelt off."

Taylor snorted. "No promises. He sounds pretty pissed." He tilted his head, giving me a meaningful look. "Now get out of here, lizard brain."

I was already halfway out the balcony door. "Hey, that one was completely unwarranted."

With one last glance back at my mate, I launched myself off the railing and shifted into my dragon form.

———

IT FELT like an eon had passed since I last spoke to my brothers. But the situation had reached a point where I felt like I *had* to talk to somebody.

Alaric's early morning fury was a blessing in disguise. Filming didn't start for a few hours, so I had time to kill. I hoped Taylor was faring well in whatever warfare Alaric waged on him...

I landed in front of the castle, shifted, then crept inside. I knew about half of my brothers would still be out cold this early in the morning, but thankfully the one I wanted to speak with was an early riser.

I found Jade's door in the library wing and knocked gently. "Hey. You awake?"

My brother opened the door. The ever-present smell of books wafted from inside, along with notes of English breakfast tea.

"Crimson," Jade said, his brows rising above his glasses. "I'm surprised to see you here."

"Me, too." I glanced over my shoulder to make sure no nosy interlopers were around.

Sensing my paranoia, Jade gestured for me to come inside. I was too restless to sit in one of the many armchairs, so I paced by the big reading nook window. Morning light reflected off the waves, but most of the island hadn't yet woken.

"I have to speak to you about something important," I said. "And I don't trust most of our lizard-brained kin to be mature about it."

Jade sounded amused. "I'm flattered. What's going on?"

I hesitated. It wasn't that I didn't want to tell Jade the truth. I knew I'd feel better once it was out, but it felt daunting to confess that I'd fallen in love with a contestant after being so vehemently against this whole reality TV idea. It was embarrassing.

"You're usually not one to be shy," Jade remarked, tilting his head. "Is something bothering you, Crimson?"

"Honestly? No. But I'm afraid *I'm* being a bother."

Jade took a sip of his tea. "How so?"

I leaned against the window and sighed. It was better to just get it out.

"I'm in love with Taylor," I said.

A silent beat passed. Jade put his tea down. The clink of the china felt loud in the quiet room.

"You... you are?" Jade asked, as if he hadn't heard correctly.

It wasn't like Jade to sound unsure of anything. He must've been startled by my confession.

"Yes."

"Are you sure?"

The hairs on the back of my neck rose. "Positive," I growled.

Jade realized I was serious. His brows rose and he sat back in his chair. "I see." A slow, genuine smile spread over his face. "Crimson, that's wonderful!"

I sighed again, some of the anxiety leaving me. "Thank you."

"So what's the problem?" Jade asked.

I gestured to the beach. "That."

"The billion grains of sand?"

"You know what I mean."

Jade took a thoughtful sip of tea. "Ah. The Dragonfate Games."

"The whole thing has been nothing but a headache," I grumbled.

"But you found your mate through it," Jade pointed out. "Knowing that, wouldn't you go through all of this again?"

I couldn't argue with that. I nodded.

"But how can the show go on?" I asked. "I already know Taylor is the one. I don't want any of those other omegas. I feel bad wasting their time. And wasting *my* precious time I could be spending with Taylor."

Jade looked unruffled, as usual. He pushed his glasses up. "Trust the process, Crimson. The whole concept of the Games isn't just to *find* your mate. It's to bond with them, too."

I hadn't thought about it that way. It was through the challenges that I'd seen Taylor's true character. His portrait had intrigued me, but it was his personality that made me fall for him.

"I suppose," I mumbled. "How many more of those idiotic challenges are there, anyway?"

My brother grinned. "Well, we planned a whole list of them—"

"Who's *we?*"

"Me and the lizard-brained gang," Jade teased. He meant the rest of our brothers.

I huffed. "I knew they had something to do with these nonsensical challenges... I can't do much more of them, Jade. For one thing, they put Taylor in danger," I growled, feeling my protective alpha instincts surge to the surface.

Jade put up a hand to calm me. "There's safeguards in place. You know we'd never let you or the contestants get hurt."

"What about when Taylor threw himself off the cliff to save his friend?"

Jade's brows rose. "He did that?"

I forgot that my brothers weren't allowed to watch the Games as they were filmed.

"Yes. If something like that happens again, I can't promise I won't intervene," I warned.

"Understandable." Jade looked amused. "And that *would* make excellent TV..."

I glared at him. "Don't put my mate in danger for that."

Jade laughed airily, dissolving my ember of anger.

"Calm down, Crimson. My, you really are smitten with Taylor, aren't you? I've never seen you act like such a nasty dragon before."

I frowned, smoothing out my suit. He was right about me usually having better control of myself. Taylor awakened my inner dragon and what it entailed—fierce protective instincts, arousal, and all.

Jade set down his tea and walked up to me, putting a comforting hand on my shoulder. "Remember that it's *your* choice in the end. No one's forcing you to pick a different omega. You can choose Taylor every single time."

"I will," I promised.

A sympathetic look flashed over my brother's gaze. "You know, the next challenge is supposed to have a dramatic finish... Perhaps we can end it after that."

Hope flared within me. "Please," I begged.

I needed the filming aspect to be over so I could ravage Taylor without an audience.

Unless he was into that.

"What do you mean by a dramatic finish?" I asked, realizing what he'd said.

He shook his head. "Can't share any more, I'm afraid. Viol would ring my neck if I spilled the details."

"*Viol* picked the next challenge?" I sputtered.

"I was just as surprised as you when he offered his input," Jade admitted. "He's oddly interested in the Games."

I couldn't imagine Viol being genuinely invested in a dating show. "He probably suggested it as a cruel joke."

Jade shrugged. "I don't know, Crimson. He was firm about getting a word in."

I rolled my eyes. "When isn't he?" Glancing out the window, I saw the sun had risen off the horizon. "Looks like the day is starting. I'd better go."

Jade nodded. "I'll do what I can to convince production to end the Games on a strong note."

I gave him a thankful nod.

As I went to leave, Jade called out, "Oh, and by the way..."

"What is it?"

He gave me a coy look. "You'd better take a shower, or douse yourself in cologne. You reek of tiger."

FIFTEEN

Taylor

_____

"YOU'RE A DIRTY CHEATER!" Alaric snapped.

I'd braced myself for a barrage of insults from the cat shifter, but that was an unpleasant way to start my day.

"Good morning to you, too," I mumbled.

"Oh, be quiet," Alaric said venomously. "Just admit it! You're lying!"

I crossed my arms. "Okay, Alaric. What exactly am I lying and cheating about?"

Alaric glared at me like he wanted me to explode. "You're cheating at the Games. And the fact that you won't own up to it is infuriating."

"How?" I shot back.

"You smell _exactly_ like Crimson. Among other lecherous things." Alaric's odd eyes flashed furiously. "I know for a fact he was here. Don't deny it."

Shit. If I lied now, Alaric would use it as ammo against me. There was no point in lying, anyway. As a fellow feline shifter, I knew Alaric's nose was as sharp as mine. He could definitely scent the _evidence_ of my late-night meeting with Crimson.

"Fine," I said quietly. "You're right."

For a second, Alaric looked shocked that I'd relented. His eyes widened before slitting into sharp knives.

"I knew it," he hissed under his breath. "You *are* cheating. You're sleeping with Crimson in order to win!"

That accusation was an irritating jab, like a nagging fly that wouldn't buzz off.

"No, Alaric," I growled. "You're right that Crimson was here last night. But I'm not trying to get any special treatment."

Alaric barked out a callous laugh. "Yeah, right! I see the way Crimson looks at you, like you're so gods-damned special. You whiff every challenge and still get chosen as the winner? I call bullshit. I *knew* something was going on behind closed doors. I should turn you in right now."

I couldn't help the one-note scoff that escaped me. That was a mistake. Alaric's face twisted into rage.

"What's so funny?" he demanded.

"Sorry. I don't think that will accomplish anything."

I meant it genuinely—I didn't want Alaric to waste his time—but my comment had the opposite effect. Alaric thought I was goading him. Apparently, he hated being on the other end of that. An angry caterwaul built in his throat. I sensed that if he was in cat form, all the hairs on his pelt would be on end. No doubt he wanted to rake his claws across my face.

It was early enough in the morning that Alaric's shouting had roused the entire floor. A couple shifters poked their heads curiously out of their rooms. Muzo yawned as he stumbled into the hall, rubbing one sleepy eye.

"What's all the ruckus?" he mumbled.

Alaric ignored him. He jabbed a finger into my chest. "Listen, tiger. I'm in love with Crimson, so do yourself a favor and back the hell off."

I was stunned into silence for a moment. Then the hilarity of his statement hit me and I laughed out loud. This, again, infuriated Alaric, who was so angry that I imagined cartoon steam coming out of his ears.

"It doesn't mean anything that you *fucked* him," Alaric snarled. "This competition is about love, not sex. And since I love Crimson, I'll be the ultimate winner."

My humor faded, replaced by anger of my own. I'd learned to deal with Alaric's crap, but hearing him insist he was in love with *my* mate was over the line. My lips curled to reveal my half-shifted tiger fangs.

"You don't love Crimson," I stated. "You think you're in love with him because you want to win."

Alaric gasped, his jaw dropping open. He reacted like I'd slapped him.

"How dare you?" he demanded.

I leaned in, challenging him back. "Tell me I'm wrong. Name a single thing about Crimson besides the fact that he's an alpha dragon."

I saw panic flicker across Alaric's face before he shook it off, glaring at me again. "I don't need to play games with you. I know I'm right. Crimson *will* choose me as the next winner. Mark my words, tiger."

"If you say so."

Alaric hated that I wouldn't rise to his bait. "I'm going to tell everyone about your trysts! Don't think you can hide it anymore!"

"Go ahead. I didn't even want to be on this stupid show," I told him.

Alaric looked offended that I'd insulted his precious Games. "Ugh. I'll never understand how a slut like you won Crimson over."

The nasty remark slid off me like oil on water. Alaric was grasping for straws, desperate to get under my skin the way

I'd accidentally slipped under his. It was kind of sad. If he wasn't such an asshole, I thought we could've gotten along.

Murmurs came from down the hall as the other contestants gossiped.

On the other hand, Muzo made no attempt to cover up his obtuse rubbernecking. "The cats are fighting!" he called.

"Shut up."

Alaric and I had spoken at the same time. We looked at each other in surprise before Alaric glared at me and stormed off like an angsty teenager.

I sighed in relief. Thank gods that was over.

Except the day had barely begun. Now the real challenge was about to start.

THE CONTESTANTS WERE UNUSUALLY tense as Gaius led us to the third challenge. I didn't know if it was because half of them had overheard my argument with Alaric that morning, or if they were just eager to win this time.

Our destination was deep in the forest. The air was fresh and thick, and the earth was loamy underfoot. Birds cried out as they flitted overhead, darting across the canopy.

Matteo, the golden eagle shifter I'd met in the previous challenge, walked next to me. He was one of the only other omegas who didn't seem tense.

"Friends of yours?" I asked, nodding to the birds.

He gave me a good-natured smirk. "You and Alaric are both cats. Is he a friend of _yours_?"

I snorted in laughter. "Fair enough."

Along with Matteo, Muzo was also eager to face the

day. That wasn't unusual for him, though. I'd never seen him nervous.

Poppy, however, trailed behind us with an ever-present mask of anxiety. I felt bad for him. It wasn't my fault that Crimson and I had fallen in love, but I still felt responsible for dragging my friends into a no-win situation. Did they even know about my relationship with Crimson? I wanted to tell them, but it wasn't the time. Confessing in front of the other contestants would be awkward, if not flat-out rude.

After what felt like an hour-long trek into the forest, Gaius finally stopped in front of a huge jutting boulder. He smiled at us and raised his arms theatrically.

"We're here at the site of our third—and final—challenge!" he declared.

Final challenge? I thought.

I wasn't the only one who was surprised. Everybody murmured in shock at what was apparently the end of the Games.

My heart flipped. Did Crimson choose to end them early because of me? That was... sweet.

"As you can see, we've gathered here deep in the forest," Gaius said. "This final challenge requires everything you've got. Strength, speed, stamina, and integrity."

I listened intently, but I also looked around for Crimson. He'd been nearby during the previous two challenges, so I assumed he was around for this one, too.

My sharp eyes caught a flicker of movement on top of the sharp boulder. A thrill ran through me when I saw Crimson standing on top of it wearing a deep hunter-green suit that blended into the forest behind him. Only the streak of red in his hair gave him away.

He met my gaze and a smile tugged at the corner of

his lips. I couldn't help but smile back. I still wasn't used to the way my heart fluttered whenever I looked at him.

A curt, impatient voice called out next to me, "What's the challenge?"

I flinched at Alaric's voice. When did he get so close to me? He must've snuck up beside me when I stared at Crimson. I noticed Alaric also staring at him. I felt a brief flicker of jealousy only for it to fade away. I wasn't threatened by Alaric at all. Crimson made it quite obvious he had no interest in him, but that didn't stop the cat shifter from craving it. I almost felt bad for him.

Gaius flashed an award-winning smile. "I'm glad you asked. Your final challenge is to hunt down a loose boar on the island."

My eyes widened in shock.

Poppy let out a small squeak. "A boar? Isn't that dangerous?"

Muzo snorted. "You're a wolf. Why are you scared of a little pig?"

"Boars aren't little," Poppy argued softly. "They're huge and have big tusks."

"Yes, they can be quite dangerous," Matteo interjected. "They're bigger than most of us here, including you, Muzo."

Muzo blinked. "Wait… They're that big?"

I sighed. "You're thinking of a barnyard pig. A wild boar is different."

Matteo glanced at me. "You're the only one here whose shifter animal can rival its size."

I mulled it over. It was true that a tiger could handle a boar better than most of the shifters here. Had Crimson chosen this task because of me?

As I glanced up to meet his gaze again, Alaric shoved past me to confront Gaius.

"That's it," Alaric snapped. "I have something to say to Crimson."

Gaius raised his brows, but was otherwise unruffled. He knew this kind of drama was excellent for TV.

"Certainly." Gaius nodded, then looked up to his friend. "Crimson, why don't you come down here?"

Crimson looked similarly surprised, but he didn't react as he leapt down from the boulder and landed gracefully on the ground. He patted off his suit.

"What seems to be the problem, Alaric?" he asked politely.

"*Him*," Alaric stated, thrusting out his arm to gesture at me. "This challenge is blatant favoritism. You know all of our shifter species by now. The only one capable of killing a boar is that tiger."

Nobody else would've noticed it, but I saw the barely perceptible flash of irritation on Crimson's face. He was annoyed that Alaric spoke of me that way. But his expression quickly returned to a calm, cordial one.

"I'm sorry you feel that way," Crimson began. "But I never said anything about *killing* the boar. Only hunting it down. All of you are capable of that, right?"

Alaric's eye twitched. Despite his anger, he knew he was being filmed. This wasn't like our incident this morning when Alaric ripped into me while the cameras were absent. He knew he couldn't argue too much with Crimson without looking bad.

But then again, he *did* have a point. It would be difficult for most of the omegas here to hunt down a boar, especially the prey animal shifters. Wasn't the point for the challenge to be difficult, though? We were supposed to prove ourselves as potential mates for Crimson.

A blush rose to my cheeks as I recalled that we'd already *mated* last night. And it was amazing. But nobody else had to know that yet—especially not Alaric. He'd spontaneously combust if he found out.

I felt a bit sorry for him. It couldn't be easy to crave an alpha's attention, to put your whole effort into earning it, not knowing whether you'd receive it or not. Despite his sour attitude, I wished the best for Alaric. Hopefully, one day he'd find an alpha who could handle him.

Unfortunately for him, that wasn't Crimson. Crimson was all mine.

"I'll tell you what, Alaric," Crimson said. "Whoever finds the boar *first* will get a guaranteed date with me."

I froze.

What did he just say?

In the past, I'd completed the challenges, but I'd never technically come in first place. I was always chosen from a pool of winners to go on dates with Crimson.

As I caught Crimson's eyes, there was a knowing gleam in them. He was calm and collected, like he knew the challenge would go according to his plans.

What did that mean for me? Did he know I'd win, no matter what? Maybe I was right when I assumed he'd tailored this challenge specifically to my skills.

My heart flipped. Crimson loved me. He promised I was the only omega he wanted, that he didn't want anybody else—and I believed him.

He *wanted* me to win.

So I'd do it.

Meanwhile, Alaric took Crimson's words as a challenge. His hands balled into fists and he nodded firmly. "Good. Look forward to our date tonight."

Without waiting to see Crimson's mildly flabbergasted expression, Alaric stormed off and shifted to prepare himself.

My friends shifted, too. Everybody was taking this challenge seriously.

Just before I shifted into my tiger form, I caught Crimson's gaze again. His ruby eyes glittered with hope. They silently seemed to say, "*I love you—and good luck.*"

SIXTEEN

Crimson

"READY... GO!" Gaius called out.

As the shifted omegas ran in all directions, my gaze was glued on Taylor. His tiger form was breathtaking. The sinuous lines of his body, his powerful yet sleek muscles, that striking black and orange coat... I couldn't take my eyes off him.

Although I'd had no input in the challenge, I silently thanked Aurum—and I guess Viol—for setting it up this way. Seeking out a wild boar in a dense forest was perfectly suited to Taylor. There was no way he'd lose.

Right?

A nagging worm of doubt entered my mind. Maybe I'd gone too far by promising a date to whoever won first. In the moment, I didn't know what else to do. He clocked my favoritism and called it out in front of everybody. I couldn't even deny it. Taylor *was* my fated mate.

But we still had a show to run. Taylor and I would be together no matter what after it ended, but what about my brothers? If there was no suspense or tension in the Dragonfate Games, would it continue to have an audience? Would contestants apply for the next season?

"What's on your mind, brother?" Gaius asked.

We stood together on the top of the jutting boulder. All the omegas had scattered into the undergrowth, and the camera crew followed them, so we were alone.

I sighed. "Did I make a mistake with that guaranteed date?"

"Not at all. It really raised the stakes." Gaius tilted his head. "But you seem to regret it."

"It's not that I regret it," I mumbled. "I just want a specific person to win. And if he doesn't..."

I trailed off, not even wanting to entertain the outcome. The idea of going on a date with somebody who wasn't Taylor made me want to gag.

"You do?" Gaius squawked.

I raised a brow at his surprise. "It's not obvious?"

"Well, call me a bird brain, but I guess not!" Gaius leaned in, whispering, "Who is it?"

That was a mild relief. I thought it was crystal-clear to everybody in the world that Taylor was my love. Then again, Gaius was a gryphon. His sense of smell wasn't as powerful as a dragon's, so he likely didn't scent Taylor all over me. Although, I had taken Jade's advice to scrub it off, then misted myself with cologne.

"You seriously don't know?" I asked.

"Is it Alaric? You two have an enemies-to-lovers vibe going on..."

I growled instinctively, deep in my chest.

Gaius laughed, slapping my shoulder. "I'm joking! Come on, Crimson, lighten up."

I removed his hand from my suit. "That is *not* funny."

Gaius's mischievous grin revealed he was screwing with me. "It's totally funny. You should've seen the look on your face! I thought you'd blast me with fire."

"I'm still thinking about it," I said, deadpan.

"It's Taylor. Am I right?" Gaius offered.

My shoulders relaxed. "Yeah."

Gaius nodded, looking pleased with himself. "I've known since the second beach date."

"That's right. You goaded me on purpose and made me lose control on TV," I grumbled.

He didn't look sorry at all. "I wanted to test how serious you were about Taylor." He grinned. "And I succeeded in proving it to you both."

I couldn't deny that was true. Taylor might not have believed my confession of love if he didn't watch—and feel—me shift into my dragon form right on top of him. And his reaction proved to me that he cared for me. *All* of me, even the animalistic, possessive dragon side.

Speaking of which, my dragon soul was pissed that Taylor was out of my sight, hidden in the forest somewhere. I wanted him where I could see him and touch him.

"You're growling, Crimson," Gaius pointed out, amused.

"Sorry."

Looking around, I heard distant crashing in the forest, but nothing too chaotic. The quiet unnerved me. I recalled what Jade said about the challenges having safeguards in place, but that didn't quell my nerves.

"Is this really safe?" I asked. "Shouldn't you be patrolling the skies or something to make sure nobody gets hurt?"

"The camera crew is with everyone."

I wrinkled my nose. "No offence to the staff, but with their size, I trust kobolds to protect the contestants as far as I can throw them."

"Isn't that pretty far?"

"Not my point. Also, the kobolds are bogged down

with cameras. They can't act like bodyguards at the same time."

Gaius tilted his head thoughtfully. "Hm, that's true."

As Gaius considered it, my skin itched with the urge to find my mate. Challenge or not, I wanted to at least see him from above, to know he was okay.

"We can cover more ground together," I said. "Come on, Gaius. It's better than standing here waiting for something to happen."

"All right, all right... You just want to see Taylor," he teased.

I didn't bother denying it.

Gaius shifted into his admittedly noble and magnificent gryphon form. For all his Hawaiian shirts and theatrical shenanigans, I sometimes forgot he took the form of a ferocious beast, too.

I shifted right after him. Gryphons were large, but nowhere close to the size of a dragon. He was about half my height.

I leapt into the air, beating my wings. Gaius joined me. His feathers softened the sound of his flapping wings, compared to the leathery snap of mine.

"You take that half of the forest, and I'll take this one," I suggested.

"Sure, boss."

We were just about to split up when a loud, piercing shriek cut through the silence.

My heart raced as terror seized me. The voice sounded feline, like a caterwaul.

Was it Taylor?

SEVENTEEN

Taylor

AS SOON AS Gaius released us, I darted into the dense undergrowth. My mind went blank except for keen focus on my task. I acted on instinct, prowling the forest on quick but silent paws.

Crimson wanted me to win.

I *would* win. There was no other option.

Still, I couldn't help the nagging memory of Crimson's promise to go on a date with the winner. He'd given up his control in the matter, leaving it up to fate—or sheer determination.

Which Alaric possessed in spades.

And if Alaric won this gods-damned challenge...

The hairs on the back of my neck rose stiffly. I was forced to swallow a growl of anger so it didn't startle the nearby forest life.

It wasn't that I didn't trust Crimson. I knew he didn't want to date anybody else. But what would Alaric do if given the opportunity to be alone with Crimson? He'd make a fool of himself. The whole thing be awkward for everyone involved...

I shook it off. I believed in Crimson, and he believed in me.

This challenge was mine to win. I had to find this boar before anybody else did.

My tiger instincts took over. All my senses came alive. My whiskers twitched, sensing minute vibrations in the air. My paw pads did the same along the earth. My nostrils took in every scent surrounding me. My sharp vision detected every tiny movement in the forest, and my ears were poised to hear any quiet snap of twigs underfoot.

Concentrate, Taylor...

It had been ages since I allowed myself to feel the way my tiger soul did. Living in a human city for so long forced me to suppress my instincts. Now I felt unleashed, like the cage locking me in had been opened.

And Crimson held the key.

Suddenly, I heard a thick, low snort.

My ears swivelled in its direction. My heart pounded. That was definitely a pig noise, and it sounded like it was going the opposite way.

Perfect.

Putting one paw in front of the other, I stalked silently towards the boar. It let out casual grunts as it rummaged around, revealing that it wasn't suspicious yet. I had the advantage.

I stepped closer. Closer...

And then a pure-white cat fell out of the sky.

Alaric rocketed down from the branch he'd been perched on, sinking his claws into the boar's back. The boar immediately squealed in rage and crashed through the bushes. All the while, Alaric clung to its back like a furry white tick.

That stupid fleabag! I thought angrily.

Swallowing a hiss, I ran after them. Not only had

Alaric ruined my chance at a clean kill, he was one step closer to victory. Finding the boar was half the challenge, one I doubted many of the remaining contestants could complete. Alaric had been smart about it.

But he wasn't about to steal my kill—*or* my date.

I pushed my muscles, running at full speed behind the rampaging boar. It wasn't just my instincts as a tiger that urged me on. A hidden wellspring of emotion flared up within me, one I now recognized as my omega instincts. They yelled at me to get that damned boar before another omega dared lay a finger on my alpha.

"Ha!" Alaric cried breathlessly from ahead. "I've got you now! I'll show you who—"

The boar squealed furiously. It took a sharp turn, then threw itself against a thick tree trunk to dislodge Alaric. I gasped as I heard his small body *thump* loudly.

"Alaric!" I called.

Before I caught up, the boar sped chaotically away. Alaric hadn't responded to my cry, but his claws still clung to the boar's fur. I didn't know if he was ignoring me on purpose, or if the impact had winded him so badly he couldn't speak.

I sped up. Challenge or not, I didn't want Alaric to get hurt, especially for a prize he ultimately wouldn't win. It would literally be an injury on top of the insult.

The boar veered erratically. This time, I saw its plan. A big boulder loomed ahead.

My stomach lurched with fear. The boar meant to crush Alaric between its thick body and the massive rock.

I sped closer, keeping pace with the boar's haunch.

"Alaric, let go!" I shouted. "It's going to kill you!"

Alaric hissed softly, but he sounded dazed. "No... I won't lose to you!"

There was no time to explain. I had to act fast.

"I know you hate me," I said. "But what's more important? Your pride, or your life?"

Alaric's eyes flashed. He was defiant, but scared. I couldn't tell if the fear was about the incoming pain, or being rejected by Crimson. I guessed both.

There was no time to think. The boar squealed. Its muscles tensed, poised to crash against the boulder and dislodge Alaric permanently. He let out a resounding caterwaul of terror.

Just before Alaric was crushed, I lunged. I grabbed him by the scruff of the neck and wrenched him off the boar's back. We tumbled off, landing in a ruffled pile of cat. The boar let out a final angry squeal, then disappeared into a dark cave ahead.

Alaric stared at me with wide eyes. His white pelt was spiked with fear. "Why did you do that?" he asked quietly.

I huffed, trying to catch my breath. "Just because you're annoying doesn't mean I want you to die."

He blinked, then aggressively licked a paw and drew it over his face to diffuse his embarrassment.

"Thanks, I guess," he mumbled.

Coming from Alaric, I'd take that as a win.

I stood up and shook out my fur. The cave the boar had disappeared into wasn't too far off. If I ran now, I'd catch it..

"Are you all right by yourself?" I asked.

Alaric made a sour face, which was a relief since he was clearly in decent enough shape to be cranky with me. He shakily got to his paws.

"I appreciate you saving my life," he grumbled, "but I'm still not letting you win."

I groaned. "Seriously? You can barely stand."

Alaric took a step forward. "I'm *fine*—" His leg gave out beneath him, and he fell face-first in the dirt with a yowl.

Empathy coursed through me. As a fellow feline, I knew how much we valued our pride. I couldn't help but feel bad for Alaric.

"I'd offer to help you, but I know you'd hate that," I said.

Alaric snorted as he got back up. "Finally, we agree on something..." He glanced at the cave. "So? What are you waiting for? Go and win."

I hesitated. "Alaric..."

"Don't pity me like that. I hate it."

"I don't pity you. I just want to tell you the truth." Twitching my tail, I gathered the words. "I'm in love with Crimson."

"Wow, what a surprise," Alaric snarked.

"And he's in love with me."

The white cat went quiet. Then he let out a long sigh. "I know that, too," he mumbled, sounding defeated.

"Then why are you trying so hard?" I asked.

Alaric lashed his fluffy tail. "What am I supposed to do? Give up on my dream?"

That took me by surprise. "Your dream?"

His fur flattened. He coughed, looking flustered. "Never mind. Forget I said anything. Go get that boar."

I put one paw forward, then paused. "Why don't you come with me?" I offered.

"I don't want your pity offering," Alaric grumbled.

"Don't be a sour puss," I grumbled right back. "What else are you going to do? Sit here and lick yourself until the challenge is over?"

Alaric considered that alternative. He apparently found it a worse outcome, because he got up and padded beside me. "Fine, let's get this over with..."

We approached the dark, yawning mouth of the cave. Even with my sharp vision, I couldn't see inside, and no sound came from within. After the boar's squealing and crashing, the forest felt unusually quiet.

"Well?" Alaric prompted. "You're the big, bad tiger. You go in."

He had a point.

I padded into the cave. As I stepped into the cool darkness, my whiskers twitched. It smelled thickly of boar, but I also caught the scent of bedding straw and milk. Was this the boar's den?

Then I heard multiple tiny sounds from deep inside the cave. It sounded like the whimpering of piglets.

A powerful, hormonal feeling engulfed me. I stepped back.

This wasn't some random wild hog running loose. This was a mother pig protecting her babies.

As I backed away, I saw a pair of glinting eyes in the darkness, followed by a loud, intimidating snort. Her brown fur camouflaged her, but the mother boar was there, daring me to take another step towards her babies.

I had no intention of doing that. Hell, if I was in her place, I'd be pissed. The thought of someone trying to harm my and Crimson's child made my fur stand on end.

When I backed out of the cave, Alaric cocked his head. "What gives? Where's the boar?" he asked.

"It's a mother boar. Her piglets are in there," I explained.

Alaric's eyes widened. That was all I needed to say. He understood, nodding. Neither of us would hunt that boar today.

Was that the real challenge all along? I recalled what Crimson said when Alaric confronted him. He specifically mentioned not killing the boar...

Suddenly, a commotion rose around us. Alaric and I watched as other contestants spilled into the clearing in front of the cave, all breathing hard and clearly ready for a fight. The closest was a gray wolf omega whose name I didn't recall, since he kept his distance from me.

"Where is it?" he demanded. "I smell the pig! I know it's here."

My hackles rose, but I didn't move yet. "Nobody's attacking the boar."

A black bear shifter leapt in to join the gray wolf. "Don't try to hide it, tiger," he growled. "You're not the only predator around here who can track prey. Move aside!"

Beside me, Alaric hissed. The gray wolf and bear paused, then burst out laughing.

"Now the pet's on your side?" the bear taunted.

"Alaric is no one's pet," I snapped. "And neither of you are touching a hair on that boar's pelt."

Alaric glanced at me, shocked that I'd stood up for him. After all our spats, I was surprised, too. But I felt an odd kinship with my fellow feline after saving his life and witnessing him being vulnerable for once.

"Then get ready for a fight," the gray wolf growled. "We're sick of watching the Taylor and Crimson show!"

I sighed and stood up on all four paws. The sooner this TV show was over, the better. It made omegas lose their damned minds. I just wanted to be in love with Crimson openly.

Could I blame the other constants, though? They wanted love. And I hoped that they would find it. But it wasn't going to happen with *my* mate.

The gray wolf and black bear stalked closer, geared for a fight. I blocked the cave entrance. Nobody was getting past me.

Then an earth-shattering roar split the sky.

My gaze snapped up. A magnificent red dragon circled overhead, then dove towards us.

My heart skipped a beat.

Crimson was here.

EIGHTEEN

Crimson

I ZONED in on the cry, desperate to reach it. My blood raced in my veins.

If anything happened to Taylor...

I cursed the canopy of trees in the way, blocking my sight. I followed the sound until I reached a clearing in the leaves. Relief washed over me when I saw that glorious orange and black coat.

I folded my wings and plummeted towards the ground. A group of shifters had gathered in front of a cave as if facing off, but my sudden appearance scattered them. I was glad for that since I didn't want to squash anybody when I landed.

"What's going on?" I asked, my voice gravelly and thick in my dragon form.

In front of me were a gray wolf and a black bear. I swivelled my head around to see Taylor and that white cat, Alaric. To my surprise, they stood side by side in front of the cave's mouth.

My heart swelled to see my mate. Warmth swam in his amber eyes. He was happy to see me, too.

"Well?" I asked when nobody responded. "I heard a loud feline scream. Is everything all right?"

Taylor and Alaric exchanged a glance. For some reason, they looked friendlier than before.

"Ah. That was me," Alaric said, flicking his tail.

I was relieved he wasn't hurt, but I was even more relieved that it hadn't been Taylor's cry.

Now that my most immediate concern was addressed, I examined the group. I'd clearly flown into the middle of a confrontation. The kobold crew lurked around the clearing, their cameras still rolling.

The black bear launched into it. "We were about to win the challenge when the tiger butted in."

"Yeah! He stopped us on purpose!" the gray wolf interjected.

A low, commanding growl rumbled in Taylor's throat. "No one is hunting that boar. Not even me."

My heart stuttered for a second. Did that mean Taylor didn't want to win the challenge?

But my fear melted as I met my mate's eyes. Fire burned in them, along with an edge of protective warmth. He wanted to win, but there was something else going on. I trusted him.

"Go on," I urged.

Taylor's tail flicked towards the mouth of the cave. "It's not just a wild boar. It's a mother. Her babies are inside that cave."

It's what? I thought, taken off guard.

Alaric narrowed his eyes and added, "So anybody who tries to get past us will get a face full of claws."

Taylor nodded at the cat. It was odd, but nice to see them getting along.

The two other predator shifters deflated.

"Well, we didn't know that," the bear grumbled.

The gray wolf shrugged. "Guess the hunt is off."

To drive the point home, they shifted back to human form. Sensing the conflict was over, Taylor did the same, as did Alaric next to him.

I was too overwhelmed by my affection for Taylor to shift, so I remained as a dragon. His courage to stand up to the other shifters for what he believed in was admirable. His omega instincts to protect children no doubt played a role, but I knew Taylor would've done the same thing even if he wasn't an omega. He was a good man.

Gaius floated down from the sky, shifting as he hit the ground. "Phew! What a plot twist!"

I raised a scaly brow. Had he known about the piglets the whole time? I didn't doubt it. That meant that, in the end, this had been a test of compassion and parental instincts, not hunting skills.

"Looks like the challenge is over," Gaius announced. "Which one of you—"

A pair of shifters crashed through the bushes, stumbling into the clearing. It was a jackal and a white wolf. I recognized them as Taylor's friends, Muzo and Poppy. They were both out of breath.

"What'd we miss?" Muzo asked, head spinning around.

Poppy sighed. "I think we're late..."

"Only a little," Gaius said, winking. "As I was saying, which one of you arrived at the boar's den first?"

As he looked around, the black bear and gray wolf shifters looked disappointedly at Taylor and Alaric. My heart squeezed. Which one of them came first? If it was Alaric, I'd have no choice but to honor my promise, and I did *not* want to do that.

But Alaric looked strangely accepting. He nudged Taylor with his elbow, which barely reached Taylor's chest.

"It was the tiger," Alaric said with the least amount of

172

venom in his voice I'd ever heard. "I was here when it happened. He discovered the cave and the piglets first."

That was a massive relief. My muscles relaxed and I let out a breath I didn't know I was holding.

Alaric glanced at Taylor like he was about to admit something else, but in the end, the two just shared a knowing look. Alaric nodded at me. "So, yeah. Stripes won, fair and square."

Taylor raised a brow. "Stripes?"

"Hey, Tay! You did it!" Muzo called excitedly.

"Yay, Taylor!" Poppy added.

I smiled at the pair. They were the least sore of all the losers, and seemed truly happy for their friend.

By now, I felt in control of myself enough to shift. "Well, Gaius?" I prompted, brushing off my suit.

He grinned and tossed the microphone at me. "You should announce the winner this time, Crimson. You seem like you have a lot to say."

I snatched the mic mid-air, then met Taylor's expectant gaze.

"For his courage and compassion, and for having the bravery to do what was right even when it might've affected the outcome of this trial... the winner of the final challenge is Taylor," I declared.

Muzo and Poppy cheered loud enough for a whole crowd.

Alaric rolled his eyes, but wore a wry smile as he golf-clapped. "Why did the rest of us even bother again?" he asked, not unkindly.

Muzo grinned. "Hey, we got a free vacation!"

I strode over to Taylor and put my hands on his waist. Finally, I could touch him the way I wanted to. I wasn't going to hide the way I felt about him any longer.

"I'm the winner of the final challenge, huh?" Taylor said coyly. "What's my reward?"

I caught Gaius from the corner of my eye. If he had anything pre-planned in mind, he didn't announce it. He nodded as if leaving the choice up to me.

In which case, I had the perfect idea.

"As the winner, your reward is... a kiss from me," I said.

Taylor blushed. We'd kissed before, but that was in private. This would be our first time kissing in front of a crowd—and on film, too. This felt different, like a bold declaration of our love.

That was exactly what I wanted. I wanted the whole world to know that Taylor was mine, forever.

My hands caressed Taylor's face. Our surroundings faded away until he was the only thing I saw. In his expression was warmth, relief, and love. He let go of his tension and embarrassment of showing affection in front of other people. He closed his eyes and leaned in.

Tilting my head, I captured his lips halfway. The softness of his mouth overwhelmed me. I threaded my fingers through his hair and cradled the back of his head in my palm as I kissed him deeper. There was no resistance or caution from Taylor. He kissed me back without a care that the entire world watched.

"Aww," Poppy murmured in the background. "They're so sweet together. I've never seen Taylor look like that..."

Muzo chuckled. "Yeah, that dragon turns him into a little kitten."

Taylor didn't stop kissing me while he flipped Muzo off.

NINETEEN

Taylor

AFTER THE COMMOTION DIED DOWN, Crimson said he wanted to show me something—away from the cameras.

The kobold director who gave him the stink eye clearly wasn't happy about that. But I was. Any time I shared with Crimson away from the hustle and bustle of the game show was a treasure.

Gaius wrapped up the challenge and sent the other omegas back to the hotel. There was a buzz of uncertainty in the air. Were the Dragonfate Games over? Crimson hadn't stuck around long enough to make an announcement. Maybe Gaius and the director would wrangle it out of him later.

For the moment, Crimson bristled with draconic energy, like invisible sparks danced along his skin. He seemed impatient and on edge, and nobody messed with him.

I loved that side of him. I wondered how much more of it I'd get to see.

Crimson practically dragged me away from the crowd into a quiet clearing in the forest, saying, "I have something to show you." I kept glancing over my shoulder to see if anyone followed, but Crimson never looked back. He was confident we'd be alone for a while.

"What did you want to show me?" I asked. "Because if it's your cock, I've already seen it."

He smirked. "No, but I can show you that, too, if you'd like."

"I'm not opposed."

He let out another laugh before tossing his head back like a rearing horse. Then a burst of magic seized him. His body grew, twisting and turning into a huge, intimidating, sexy form.

Crimson's dragon stood before me. There wasn't a single frightened bone in my body, but I saw how somebody could find him menacing. For one thing, he was massive, nearly the size of a bungalow. His hooked black talons could rip up a car with ease, and his shiny fangs glinted like a row of knives.

This wasn't my first time seeing his dragon form, yet it never dulled my awe. I reached out and touched my palm to his foreleg. The red scales were smooth and cool under my hand.

No, calling them *red* was an understatement. True to his name, they were a rich crimson, drifting into a different shade at various angles of the light. He was like a living, breathing ruby statue with lungs full of fire.

And he was mine.

A shiver ran through me. Just as Crimson was possessive over me, I was possessive over him. The end of the challenges came as a relief.

"Don't ever do that shit again," I muttered.

Crimson's dragon voice rumbled with amusement. "Do what, my sweet kitten?"

"Threaten to go on a date with some other omega."

Scoffing, Crimson brought a paw to his chest in an offended gesture. "I did no such thing. I knew from the start you'd win, Taylor. Have faith in your alpha."

"I do have faith in *you*. It was everyone else I didn't have faith in. Could you imagine going on a TV show date with one of those guys? The second-hand cringe would be unbearable."

He laughed. "You're not wrong. I would've fought the urge to set myself on fire." Craning his neck toward the ground, he nuzzled my cheek with his smooth muzzle. "You don't have to worry about that anymore. The Games are over. You're my mate, Taylor, and I love you."

Those words made my heart flutter every single time.

"Now stop thinking about silly things and get on my back," Crimson said.

"Get *where?*"

"How else am I supposed to take you to the castle? It's a long walk for someone without wings."

As a tiger, I wasn't exactly afraid of heights. I could climb a tree well enough.

But being in the *sky?*

Sensing my hesitation, Crimson let out a puff of smoke. "Come on. Do you really think I'd let you fall?"

"I'm not that light," I warned him.

"And I'm not that weak," he shot back. Then he sighed dramatically. "Honestly, Taylor. It's like you've never met a dragon before! We're only the strongest creatures in existence."

I rolled my eyes. "And the most pompous. Let me on."

"I was kidding about getting on my back, by the way. Far too dangerous, especially since you might be pregnant."

My jaw dropped. What did he just say?

Crimson kept speaking like he hadn't just dropped a

huge bombshell. "I've made a neat little seat for you. And I promise on the lives of my six brothers that I won't drop you. Wait, no. I promise on my tail I won't—"

"Crimson," I interrupted. "Did you say I might be pregnant?"

He didn't look nearly as shocked as I felt. "Well, yes, certainly. We had unprotected sex, didn't we?"

"Yes..."

"We even talked about it, remember? I said, 'I want to breed you, Taylor.' And you said, 'Put an egg in me.'"

My face turned hotter than the sun. I *did* say that. I'd been caught up in the heat of the moment, the sultry dirty talk.

But that wasn't all it was. In my heart, everything I'd said was true.

There was a distinct possibility that our intercourse had resulted in pregnancy. Of course I knew that. I was a grown man who knew how biology worked. But this whole experience felt so surreal, so dreamlike, that I hadn't considered that fact. It was like I was untouchable here on Chromatimaeus Island.

I slowly looked down at my body, seeing it with a new perspective. I placed my hands on my belly. It felt the same as ever, so maybe it was my imagination kicking in when I thought it seemed different than before.

But a whole new world opened up in my mind. A vision of me, pregnant. Crimson as the father. And a beautiful baby between us...

Tears sprung to my eyes.

"Taylor, are you all right?" Crimson asked softly.

"Yeah." I was so choked up I could barely talk. My voice was thick with emotion.

Crimson hesitated. When he spoke, he sounded worried. "You're not upset, are you?"

"No, you overgrown lizard," I half-snapped, half-sobbed. "I'm happy!"

Instantly relieved, Crimson wrapped his long neck around me, cuddling close with a grin. "Aww, look at you. Underneath that prickly exterior, you're a big softie, aren't you?"

I sniffled loudly. "I'm going to claw your face off."

Crimson beamed like I'd complimented him. "Yes, yes. Now come on, let's have our celebration somewhere a little more luxurious."

IT TURNED out I was too distracted to be scared of heights. The whole time Crimson flew us back to his family's castle, my mind raced with thoughts of our potential baby. I'd been so busy with my rivalry-turned-sort-of-friendship with Alaric, the challenges, and the chaos of reality TV, that the unprotected sex had slipped my mind.

Was there a dragon egg forming inside of me right now?

My heart skipped a beat. I hoped so. And if there wasn't, nothing stopped me and Crimson from trying over and over again.

"There it is," Crimson said.

Since he clutched me securely in his paws against his chest, I felt the deep rumble of his voice against my back.

It wasn't hard to miss the castle, but that didn't stop my sense of wonder. I was a city boy, whether I liked it or not, so the sight of a beautiful, edgy castle on a forested island took my breath away. It was like a visual out of a film.

I couldn't voice my awe, so instead I said, "I don't envy your house cleaner."

That earned me a cackle from Crimson.

He touched down by the looming front doors on a cobblestone walkway. The area looked both well-manicured and untamed, like the castle was a natural extension of the wilderness. It was a fitting home for dragons—creatures who were noble and smart, yet harbored a ferocious feral side.

After placing me gently on the ground, Crimson shifted back to human form and adjusted his suit. "Here we are. Home."

My chest felt warm. Was this to be my home, too?

"Is this what you wanted to show me?" I asked.

"Not quite. Follow me."

Entering the castle felt like stepping into another world. I was no lithe little omega, but the arched ceilings, at least ten feet high, made me feel small. Was this castle built with the dragon brothers in mind so they could take either form they pleased?

Yet for a castle housing six other dragons, it was surprisingly empty.

"Where is everybody?" I asked as Crimson led me up a flight of stairs.

"What am I, a babysitter?" Crimson teased. "Jade is locked up in his library, no doubt. I suspect the twins, Aurum and Saffron, are sneaking around production to get a glimpse of the action. Thystle is probably moping in his room listening to My Chemical Romance, while Cobalt is undoubtedly doing serious adult dragon things that none of us are privy to or care about."

From his list, I only counted six, including Crimson.

"What about the seventh brother?" I asked.

A silent beat passed before he answered. "Best not to guess with Viol. He's a wild card."

The way he said it made me think he didn't want to discuss that particular brother further, so I let it slide.

After many long hallways, we reached a pristine red door. Crimson opened it and gestured for me to enter.

What I expected was—well, a bedroom. What I got was a massive, sprawling space the size of a penthouse suite. Calling it a 'room' was like calling a mansion a house.

That wasn't all, though. As I took in the scale of his room, Crimson wandered over to another door and beckoned me closer. This one had a different aura. The deep cherry wood was hand-carved with intricate designs, secured with a numbered digital padlock.

"What's that for?" I asked.

"So my snooping brothers and house staff don't enter."

"Is this the part where I get concerned about dead bodies?"

"No, because I'd let my brothers see those," he joked. Maybe.

Crimson punched in the key code with quick, practised movements, but he didn't open the door right away. He paused at the threshold, smoothing back his hair and taking a deep breath.

"You okay?" I asked.

Crimson bounced on the balls of his feet. "Yes."

"...Are you sure?"

He shot me a playful glare. "Listen, it's a big deal to show off your hoard to your mate for the first time."

My eyes widened. I hadn't realized his hoard lay behind this door. I had to admit, the concept of dragon hoards hadn't meant much to me until I met Crimson. His passion for his collection of suits went beyond a normal person's interest. It was kind of like what quilting meant to me.

I put my hand reassuringly on his arm. "I know how important it is to you."

The tension eased from Crimson's face. "Hah. How embarrassing of me. Of course my mate would understand."

I smiled, then leaned up to give him a kiss on the cheek for good measure. He replied with a loving growl, a less-than-chaste kiss in return, and a possessive grab of my ass. Being so close to his hoard must've awakened his dragon instincts, making him wilder than usual, which was fine by me.

With a deep breath, Crimson opened the door.

Much like the castle, the sight of Crimson's meticulously kept and displayed hoard instilled a sense of awe in me. Rows of suits lined the deep, wide walk-in closet, which was nearly the size of a room itself. Pot lights and rows of stealthily placed LED strips shone down from above, casting the suits in an ethereal glow, while the black closet walls created a cozy atmosphere. There wasn't a single speck of dust on any of the fabric. It was clear Crimson's hoard was handled with painstaking, meticulous care.

When I glanced at him, he almost looked embarrassed.

"What's up?" I asked.

"You're not going to laugh?" He sounded like he half-expected me to.

I raised a brow, crossing my arms. "Crimson, my main hobby is quilting. You know, the thing usually associated with little old ladies with nothing better to do. Which is ridiculous, since it's dismissive of the whole art form, but whatever..." I gestured to the suits. "So as a fellow connoisseur of fabric—*and* your mate, might I remind you—why the hell would you think I'd shame you for this?"

Crimson blinked, shocked by my impassioned speech, then let out a relieved laugh. "You're right. That was silly of me." He glanced at the door, which he shut behind us.

"You know, I don't let my brothers in here. Jade came in earlier this week by accident and I nearly bit his face off. Nobody else is allowed... except you."

That made me feel oddly special. "Thank you for trusting me, Crimson."

He grabbed me by the waist, pulling me against him. "Thank *you* for being my perfect mate."

As we hugged, I couldn't help noticing the closest suit hanging on the rack. I couldn't identify the material at a glance, so my fabric nerdiness bubbled to the surface.

"Is that cotton, or a silk blend?" I asked.

Crimson grinned at my interest. "Neither. It's Merino wool."

"Really? But it's so smooth and shiny."

My alpha chuckled, nuzzling my face with great fondness. "Ah, you really *are* my fated mate, Taylor."

TWENTY

Crimson

_____

THERE WAS one nagging thing on my mind as we exited my closet. After Taylor was so honest and accepting of my hoard, I felt encouraged to bring it up with him.

"So, now what?" Taylor asked. "Castle tour? Meeting the family? Wrapping up the game show?"

"Why, are you in a hurry to escape me?" I teased.

Taylor shot me a deadpan look. "Yes, almighty lizard. I tremble before you."

"Call me a lizard again and see if my boner stays alive."

Intrigued, Taylor's gaze fell to the front of my pants. A slow grin spread over his face.

"You should've just said so," he mumbled as he sauntered over. But before Taylor wrapped his arms around me, I raised a hand. He paused. "What is it?"

I glanced hesitantly at my closet, then back at my mate. "There's something I want to try."

"I'm listening."

A bead of sweat rolled down my temple and my palms turned clammy. Getting out my request proved harder than

I expected, but I should've known it would be hard when it was so dreadfully lewd...

Taylor raised a brow as my silence went on. "Crimson, do you have some kind of kink you're scared to share with me?"

My face flushed. "I beg your pardon?"

But he was nonplussed. "You can tell me. Fated mates and all that, remember? Didn't I just tell you literally five minutes ago not to be ashamed of things you enjoy?"

I sighed, worn down by his stoic sensibility. "Yes, I know. But this is different."

"I doubt that."

"Does *anything* faze you, my love?"

"Not really. Except realizing I might be pregnant. But that was in a good way."

There was no point in hiding the truth any longer. Just because *I* found my little fantasy embarrassing didn't mean Taylor would.

"So? What's this non-vanilla kink you have?" Taylor pried.

"In the grand scheme of things, it's not that wild. But it has to do with my precious hoard, so I'm a bit nervous," I admitted.

Taylor smiled sympathetically. "Sure. If you want, let's explore it together. Tell me more about
it."

I swallowed. The image of it in my mind was very hot, but would I feel the same way in real life? There was no better way to find out than what Taylor had suggested— exploring it together.

I bit my lip.

"I, ah... want you to come on my suit," I murmured.

Taylor's brows shot up. He looked genuinely surprised.

"Oh. That's it? I thought you were into diapers or something."

I chuckled. "And what if I was?"

"For you, I'd try anything once."

The unexpectedly sweet comment made me smile. I held him close, wrapping my arms around him like a baby koala, never wanting to let go.

Taylor's scent was musky and thick, and his soft neck practically begged for me to bite it. But if I went down that road, it would lead to full-on fucking again. Not that there was anything wrong with that, but I wanted to try something different.

As we embraced, I let my hand roam down Taylor's chest, finally resting on the slight bulge in the front of his pants. He purred, which was adorable.

"Do dragons always get horny over their hoard?" he asked.

"I don't know. I never thought of my hoard that way until I met you. Perhaps our fated mates unlock kinks related to our hoard."

Taylor swallowed audibly. "Someone should do a study on it."

Despite trying to keep his voice steady, I heard it hitch. It was cute when his stoicism crumbled under erotic pressure.

I kept caressing his growing erection. Taylor closed his eyes as his breathing quickened, along with the rise and fall of his chest. I felt his beating heart rapidly thumping against mine.

"Already pent up since last night?" I teased.

"Sorry that it feels good when an alpha dragon feels me up," Taylor grumbled, his cheeks deep pink.

"Let's take care of that, shall we?"

With a deft motion, I slipped my hand beneath the

waistband of his pants and pulled out my throbbing prize. Taylor gasped. The sudden sensation of cool air against his hot cock made him shiver.

I licked my lips. My mate's cock was gorgeous. A shiny bead of pre-cum glistened at the tip of his swollen head. My mouth watered, eager to engulf it.

But as I began to kneel down, Taylor grabbed my shoulders.

"Don't," he said in a strained voice.

"Hm? Why not?"

He mumbled the next words, clearly embarrassed. "I'm already close. I won't be able to hold back and... come on your suit."

A wave of fondness hit me. "Aww, Taylor. You're too sweet."

"Whatever," he grumbled, as red as my dragon's scales.

I kissed him to diffuse his embarrassment. Soon, he was lost in our passionate make-out and threw his shame to the wind, moaning and whimpering into my mouth. My mate's lustful sounds sent shockwaves of arousal rocketing through my body. My cock ached.

Taylor pulled back from our kiss. His eyes flashed, glassy and mischievous. He glanced down at my blazer, then gently ran his hands over it.

"Such fine fabric," he murmured.

My heart skipped a beat, and my hand paused on Taylor's shaft.

His ferocious tiger eyes glinted again. He knew he just hit the jackpot.

"You like that, don't you?" he asked softly as his fingers dragged down the fabric. "You like when I compliment your suit."

A lump formed in my throat. I couldn't speak. I nodded, my head swimming.

Taylor smirked. "That's adorable. Don't forget to keep touching me. Unless you're so horny that you can't move."

My brain fired off a few weak motor neurons, but my pace wasn't nearly as steady as before. I was too distracted by Taylor's gentle, fabric-respecting touch and his dirty compliments.

"This suit looks so sexy on you," Taylor murmured. When his fingers slipped into the inner lining of the blazer's pocket, I gasped as if he'd penetrated me. "What is this? Silk?"

I nodded again, too aroused to formulate even a single-word reply.

"So delicate and smooth. You don't even put anything in these pockets, do you, Crimson? It would sully them."

I felt like my head was going to explode. First of all, how the hell did he know that? Second of all, why was this experience so hot?

"Hm, if that's how you feel... then maybe I shouldn't do *this*."

I glanced down to see Taylor readying two fingers just outside the hem of my pocket, then froze as he plunged them inside. I whimpered, biting my lip. He wasn't even touching me, just my clothes, but it felt as good as if he'd thrust his fingers into my ass. My body trembled as I lost my wits. I used my remaining capacity to work Taylor's cock with my shaky hand. It wasn't the best handjob I'd ever given, but it was all I could do right now while Taylor turned me into mush.

As Taylor finger-fucked my suit pocket, he leaned in to whisper in my ear. "You really like this, don't you? Having your precious suit defiled like a slut?"

I bit down hard on my lip to stop myself from coming instantly. I nodded frantically.

"I'm barely doing anything, yet you're a whimpering

mess," Taylor said casually. "In fact, why don't I double-penetrate you?"

A tiny whine escaped me. If he did both pockets, I didn't know if I'd be able to keep standing.

But Taylor didn't relent. Using his broad chest to keep me stable, he slipped his other hand down to my opposite side. I watched with bated breath, my heart pounding like a stampede of horses.

"Look, Crimson," Taylor ordered.

"I'm looking," I promised in a weak whisper.

He grinned. "Oh, so you can still talk after all."

"I *am* a dragon," I said with a huff. "It'll take more than that to—"

Taylor prepared three fingers, then thrust them into my second virgin pocket.

I cried out. A psychosomatic lust seized me. I felt frenzied, like Taylor was fucking my hole with a ten-inch dildo instead of putting his fingers in my blazer. My knees nearly gave out as I fell forward, desperately clutching him with my free hand. I had to focus on Taylor's handjob or I'd lose my mind. Hell, I was most of the way there already.

But as Taylor's fingers thrust in and out of my silk pockets, my movements grew pitiful and weak. My skull felt full of cotton. I could barely think. All I felt was overwhelming arousal pulsing in my veins.

Taylor pulled his hands out. I stood there, gasping for breath.

"Sit on the edge of the bed," Taylor ordered.

I stumbled over and obeyed him. I didn't know what he was going to do, so I watched him closely while catching my breath.

But that didn't last long. Taylor approached me with his hard, pulsing cock in hand.

"Crimson," he said.

Thank Holy Drake I'd collected enough air to speak. "Yes?"

"Does your suit have an inner pocket?"

My jaw dropped.

No... he wasn't going to...

After my long, dumbfounded, pin-drop silence, Taylor asked again. "Crimson. Inner pocket?"

"Yes," I said in a small, tinny voice.

"Present it for me, please."

With a shaky hand, I slowly drew open the front of my blazer, exposing the silk lining inside. I felt beyond exposed. Vulnerable. It was deeply erotic.

Taylor's cock bobbed in the air as he stepped closer. It was inches from my suit. My heart pounded a mile a minute, thundering so hard it felt like it would burst from my ribs. I'd never been in such a haze of lust before. Sharing my hoard with my mate this way was intimate. Nobody else was allowed to even touch my hoard... but I wanted Taylor to dirty it with his cock. Maybe that's what made this all so sexy.

"Keep it open for me, please," Taylor said.

Grasping the base of his cock, he inched it closer. I was frozen, barely able to breathe. When the tip of his head brushed against the pocket hem, I bit back a moan. How could this feel so good? My cock throbbed almost painfully in my pants, my balls swollen and aching.

Taylor moved his dick up and down, teasing the pocket entrance like it was a bodily hole. My heart leapt into my throat when I saw a dark smear of pre-cum on the fabric. He'd already left a mark on my precious suit—and all it did was turn me on harder.

"I'm going in now," Taylor said. "Are you ready?"

"Y-yes."

"Are you sure? We can stop if you don't like it."

I glared at him, a draconic hiss escaping my teeth. When I was in an overly aroused state like this, it was easier for my dragon side to burst forth.

It amused Taylor. "Okay, I get it. Now hold still so I can fuck you."

I stilled myself. My hands grasped the bed covers for dear life.

The head of Taylor's cock slowly, gently parted the opening of the pocket. I let out a ragged breath. Watching his cock open it up like that was so hot. He swirled it around near the entrance, as if stretching the hole. I clenched my teeth so I wouldn't cry out.

Then Taylor rocked his hips forward, plunging his hard cock into my inner pocket. This time I couldn't hold back. A cry escaped me, loud and desperate. Why did this feel so fucking good?

Taylor's breaths turned ragged, too. He canted his hips, thrusting in and out of my silk pocket in a steady rhythm. I felt the weight and girth of his cock like it was physically inside my body. Sweat dripped down my temples, and my cheeks burned. I was beyond flustered.

Taylor grunted with effort as his thrusts sped up. "You love having your suit defiled like this, don't you?"

"Yes," I whimpered.

"Good."

His thrusts grew erratic and sloppy. Once in a while his cock slipped out of the pocket so he'd shove it back in, which drove me wild. His balls slapped against the fabric as he pushed the whole length of his throbbing cock into it. Taylor hissed through his teeth. He looked badly flustered, too. I wondered how close he was to his limit.

"Do you want to touch yourself?" Taylor asked. "Do it."

My hand scrambled eagerly for my cock. I worked it haphazardly, too dazed to give it any thought or skill.

Taylor groaned. "I'm close. Where do you want me to finish? Inside..." He traced a finger down the front of my blazer. "Or on top?"

Fuck, I mentally screamed. Both were such good options.

"On... on top," I finally decided.

"All right," Taylor said, still fucking my pocket. "Watch me come all over your suit, Crimson."

"Yes," I breathed.

Pulling away after a final deep thrust, Taylor worked his cock for a few more quick strokes. Then his whole body tensed. He roared, clenching his eyes shut as his cock twitched violently, then erupted in thick white spurts all over the front of my blazer. I was mesmerized and stupid with lust. I jerked myself off mindlessly at the scene until I peaked, careening over the edge. A massive orgasm hit me like a truck. I arched my back and screamed, my voice cracking. I felt my warm cum shoot out in jets and drip down my hand, coating it and my pants for good measure.

When it was over, I collapsed on the bed, thankful Taylor had led me there. If I'd done that standing up, I would've definitely passed out and hit my head on the floor. I gasped for breath throughout the dizzying aftershocks.

Taylor slumped next to me, looking equally worn but satisfied.

"Gonna assume that you liked that," he said breathlessly.

I snorted. "Yes, I hope that much was obvious."

Rolling over, I pulled him into my grasp. My instincts craved post-sex physical contact. I growled possessively into

Taylor's neck. If I was any less exhausted, I might've bitten him again.

"It's official," Taylor said, sounding amused. "You have a suit kink."

I sighed. "I suppose I do. Thank you for unlocking it with me."

"What are fated mates for?" he said with a grin.

As we cuddled on the bed, a sudden slam of the door interrupted our peaceful silence.

Aurum's obnoxious voice shattered the calm as he called, "Hey, Crimson, are you—" He stopped dead in his tracks, blinking at us in sudden understanding. "Oh. Hi."

I shot him the mother of all death glares. Unfortunately, being my annoying younger brother, he was immune to it.

"Well, well, well," Aurum said, pleasantly smug. "What do we have here?"

Taylor flushed, quickly trying to cover himself so he didn't accidentally flash this stranger.

"Nah, don't bother," Aurum said casually, waving it off. "After all, we're family now, right?"

"I'm sorry, I don't remember inviting you here," I snapped.

But it had no effect. He was too pleased with himself to notice my irritation. "I recall a certain brother of mine being sooo opposed to the Dragonfate Games," Aurum sneered. "And now look at him, curled up in bed with his sweetheart!"

"Keep talking and I'll turn you into dragon soup," I warned.

"I'm assuming this is one of your brothers," Taylor said wryly. He seemed profoundly less annoyed than I was.

"Yes, unfortunately. That's Aurum, one of the twins."

Taking this as his cue to say hi, Aurum strode up to the bed. "Pleased to meet you, Mr. Tiger!"

I groaned loudly. "Don't come over here, you idiotic lizard."

But Aurum just grinned. I knew he was too interested in Taylor to back off, no matter what kind of violence I threatened him with. I might as well let it happen.

"I'd shake your hand, but, uh..." Aurum snickered. "You know."

Taylor's face remained stoic, but his blush was clear as day. "My apologies."

"Nah, I'm glad Crimson finally got some."

"I'm two seconds away from committing fratricide," I warned him. "Wasn't there something you had to say?"

Aurum nodded. "Oh, yeah. We've been looking all over for you. Duke wants you at the closing ceremonies. Y'know, since you found your mate and the Games are over." He put a hand to his chest. "Which you should *personally* thank me for. By the way, you guys are a super cute couple."

"First of all, the Games were Saffron's idea, not yours, you little liar. Second..." I sighed, then muttered, "thank you, I suppose."

Aurum's jaw dropped. "Crimson? Thanking me? Wow, Taylor. You've really changed him in a short amount of time."

"I try," Taylor said, shooting me an impish glance.

"Yes, yes, Crimson is a big, bad salty dragon," I grumbled. "Now can you get the hell out of my room?"

I took a playful swipe at Aurum, which he dodged thanks to his lanky body. "Don't forget to shower before filming!"

TWENTY-ONE

Taylor
─────────

AFTER A JOINT SHOWER in Crimson's luxurious, private-spa-like bathroom, we headed back to the beach where the closing ceremonies were being held. Unlike any other Games-related event, I wasn't anxious about this one. I felt calm and peaceful, but it was also kind of bittersweet that it was over. I'd looked forward to the end the whole time, and now that it was finally here, it felt surreal.

Crimson landed in his dragon form away from the crowd, then shifted so we could walk over to the main stage together. But Duke, the gruff kobold director, seemed silently pissed that Crimson had been mysteriously absent for so long. Every camera was shoved in our faces, soaking up as much of our hand-holding as possible. Knowing it would be over soon made it bearable, so I just attempted to smile and wave.

Crimson took the whole thing in stride. He flashed grins to every camera lens and made a big show of holding my hand and affectionately bumping my shoulder. I'd never been on the receiving end of PDA before, so this experience was a crash course.

We leapt onto the platform where Gaius waited for us.

His shirt-du-jour was a bright pink button-up with red hibiscus flowers printed all over it, as if to highlight the romantic mood. Unlike Duke, who glowered behind his camera, Gaius was genuinely excited to see us. He hugged both of us. Before pulling away, he whispered to Crimson, "Nice catch." Then he winked at me and resumed his role of host.

"Well, folks, it's been a whirlwind, thrilling journey, but we've finally reached the conclusion of the Dragonfate Games!" Gaius strode across the stage, commanding the attention of the crowd—and the audience who would eventually watch this at home. "Before we begin, I'd like to thank *all* the contestants for joining us on this incredible ride."

As he spoke, I glanced at the people on the beach. All the omegas from the Games were there, including the ones who'd lost earlier challenges. Among the familiar faces were my friends—Poppy, Muzo, Matteo, and I guess that included Alaric now, too. Poppy and Matteo smiled, Muzo waved, and Alaric shot me a knowing glance, like he was ready for Gaius to embarrass me on stage by gushing about my love for Crimson.

Gaius gestured to the small crowd of contestants. "You may not have won the dragon's heart, but you gave it your all. Any alpha would be pleased to have you."

He sounded so genuine that it was hard to believe he was a reality TV host. A sudden thought hit me. Gaius was an alpha, too, wasn't he? He'd never mentioned having a mate. Was there a possibility he was interested in one of the contestants?

"As a reward for taking a chance on the Dragonfate Games, you all have an open invitation to return again next season!" Gaius announced.

A good chunk of the crowd exploded into excited murmurs.

"Next season?" Alaric asked, eyes widening.

Gaius nodded. "That's right. In fact... come on out here, everyone!"

I looked around, confused. I'd met Aurum earlier, but I didn't see him anywhere, or anyone else who looked like he might be Crimson's brother. Where could Gaius hide six alpha dragons?

When I glanced at Crimson for answers, he shrugged. Apparently, he didn't know either.

But then I *heard* them.

The leathery snap of wings—many pairs of wings—alerted me to their arrival. I stared up at the sky, mouth agape at the sight. Five dragons of various sizes and shades descended from the air. Their scales glittered with every color of the rainbow. The two smallest ones were gold and yellow. Two medium-sized dragons followed, one a lush green and the other pale indigo. The dragon furthest back was the largest. He was deep blue, like a living creature made up of the ocean itself.

Awed sounds came from the crowd. The camera crew swivelled around, getting perfect shots of the dragons' descent.

It all only lasted a few seconds. The dragons were fast. It felt like I blinked and then the huge, scaly beasts had shifted mid-air, landing on the stage beside us as handsome alpha men.

"Talk about an overly dramatic entrance," Crimson mumbled to me.

I noticed one was missing. Judging by their hair colors, it must've been Viol, the mysterious brother Crimson wasn't keen on talking about. I assumed he wasn't participating in the future Games.

"Welcome, dragons, and thank you for that delightful display," Gaius said.

Since he always talked in a playful tone, I couldn't tell if he was teasing them or not. Judging by the looks on some of the brothers' faces, it didn't seem the grand entrance was their idea. I wondered if production had put them up to it to stir up hype for the next season.

And it worked. The omegas stared up at the alpha brothers with great interest—some of them more than others. For one, Alaric looked ready to jump someone's bones. As I glanced back and forth between my friends and Crimson's brothers, I wondered if they would find love here on this island, too, just like I did.

I tightened my grip on Crimson's hand. He squeezed me back gently.

Gaius went on to thank the team and put a tidy figurative bow on the whole season. As charismatic as he was, I tuned him out. I couldn't help being distracted by some of the curious glances Crimson's brothers shot my way. It was my first time seeing most of them, so I figured the curiosity was mutual. But a few of the brothers seemed more interested in omegas among the crowd. That was fine by me. All the attention was too much for my tastes. And hey, if my friends found a sexy alpha dragon mate on this ridiculous game show one way or another, I was all for it.

After what felt like ages of TV formality, Gaius turned to me and Crimson one last time.

"Well, you two? How about wrapping it up with a nice kiss for the viewers at home?" he suggested.

I blushed. Talk about PDA cranked up to the max.

"*Finally*, Gaius," Crimson quipped as he grabbed my waist. "I thought you'd never ask."

My mate dipped me low and brought his face closer to mine. As soon as our lips met, all my shame faded away.

All I cared about was the warmth of my mate's mouth. I let Crimson kiss me in front of a dozen cameras to the background noise of cheering and whooping.

AFTER FILMING OFFICIALLY ENDED, I caught up with my friends. Their flight home was the next morning, so I wanted to speak with them before they left.

I crushed Muzo and Poppy in a big hug. I wasn't typically so overtly affectionate, but Crimson turned me into a sap. Either that, or it was my pregnancy hormones flaring up early.

"Ack... can't... breathe," Muzo squeaked.

Poppy sniffled, crying for a different reason. "I'm so happy for you, Taylor, but I'm going to miss you so much... Will I ever see you again?"

"Of course, Poppy. Besides, I still have business to wrap up in the city before I move here permanently."

Muzo gasped, ignoring my entire statement. "Tay! You're gonna be stranded on this island forever! I'm never gonna visit your weird apartment again!"

"I'm not stranded. And how is my apartment weird?" I mumbled, still hugging him as he sobbed.

Alaric rolled his eyes as he strolled closer. "Dear gods, you two are dramatic. Didn't you hear a word Gaius said? We have an invitation to return next season. I'll be here."

"I think I'll return, too," Matteo added, shooting an amused glance at the wailing omegas in my arms. "It wasn't Crimson, but I'm not convinced my mate isn't here on this island. Call it eagle's intuition."

Alaric glared at him. "Just don't get in my way."

"Of course. As long as you don't get in mine, either," Matteo said with a friendly smile.

I snorted. "Can you keep your claws sheathed next season, Alaric? Or will I have to supervise you?"

"You can supervise my ass," the cat retorted.

I grinned, pleased to be on Alaric's good side. Probably.

After saying goodbye to everybody, Crimson pulled me aside. "How do you feel, my love? Not out of social energy, I hope?" he asked.

"Let me guess," I replied. "I have five of your brothers to officially meet."

He grinned. "Yes, but they can wait if you're tired. Though, I can't promise *some* of them won't barge in on us in their excitement to meet you."

I kissed Crimson on the cheek. "Thanks, but I'm fine. I'd love to meet them."

As the sun began its slow, summery descent into the horizon, it turned everything a beautiful shade of gold. With the staff and contestants gone, the private island felt like another world. The beach was empty except for me, Crimson and five of his brothers.

Aurum grinned and waved as we approached. At least, I thought it was Aurum. He and his identical twin were impossible to tell apart, especially in this golden hour.

Crimson held my hand and cleared his throat. "Well, I suppose it's time you met the family. You've met half of the twins, Aurum and Saffron." He gestured to the others, going in order from the youngest to oldest. "Thystle, Jade, and Cobalt." He didn't bother mentioning Viol, who was absent. "Everybody, this is—"

"Wait, wait, wait," Aurum interrupted.

Crimson glared at him. "What?"

Aurum wagged a finger. "Not so fast, Mr. This Is Undoubtedly The Worst Idea Anyone In The History Of The Planet Has Ever Had."

I turned to Crimson in confusion. My mate had a scrunched, pouty expression, like someone called out for a crime committed long ago. Meanwhile, the twin alpha dragons grinned expectantly.

"Well, Crimson?" Aurum crossed his arms. "Why don't you tell Saffron what you told me?"

"You've clearly already told him," Crimson grumbled.

"But we want to hear *you* say it."

After a moment of internal debate, Crimson let out a long, haggard sigh. But I noticed a tiny smirk in the corner of his mouth. "Fine. Thank you, Saffron, for this inane, asinine dating show idea. Despite its ridiculous nature, it allowed me to find my one true love, who is likely now pregnant, and—"

"Pregnant?" Jade, the one with glasses, echoed.

Thystle sputtered, his fluffy bangs moving to reveal both wide eyes. "*Pregnant?*"

Cobalt said nothing, but his stoic expression shifted slightly.

Ignoring the gawking twins, the three older brothers rushed over to congratulate us. From the corner of my eye, I saw Crimson flash a smug grin at the twins. He'd done a fantastic job snaking out of that public sibling argument. The two stewed silently for a second, no doubt plotting their later revenge, then dropped it in favor of joining in the family's excitement.

"Welcome to the family, Taylor," Jade said warmly.

"Yeah, it's cool to have a tiger among us," Thystle added with a grin.

When Cobalt spoke for the first time, the deep timbre of his voice surprised me. "Are you well? How is the baby?"

"We don't know for sure if I *am* pregnant yet," I admitted.

Crimson grinned, hugging me closer. "Don't be so modest, my love. There's a very distinct chance. And if not now, then..."

Aurum and Saffron groaned, then spoke at the same time. "We get it, you fuck."

Jade chuckled. "Don't mind the twins. They're just as eager about you and the baby as the rest of us, but they have a score to settle with Crimson."

I nodded. "I figured."

Crimson slipped his arm around me. "It's been a long day. Ready to head home?"

I rested my head on his shoulder in response. "Ready."

TWENTY-TWO

Crimson

THE NEXT MONTH brought two incredibly exciting developments.

First was the fact that Taylor's belly began to swell with my egg.

Second was the delivery of Taylor's belongings—most importantly, his completed quilts, supplies, and his beloved sewing machine.

Since Gaius frequently flew to and from Chromatimaeus Island, he took on the responsibility of arranging a shifter moving company to do the work. When Taylor's belongings arrived, safe and sound, he cried silent tears of joy, rubbing them away on his sleeve so nobody would see.

"I've missed you so much," he murmured to his solid metal sewing machine, stroking its chassis like a lover.

"Should I be jealous?" I joked as Taylor set it up in its own corner of the bedroom.

He shot me a wry look. "They haven't invented sewing feet that double as dildos, so no."

"Very funny."

After we finished unpacking his quilting supplies, Taylor blew out a breath. He sounded tired already, which didn't surprise me. Dragon eggs grew fast, and it must've been harder on his body since he wasn't a dragon.

I gently dragged Taylor away from the quilting corner and sat him down on the bed.

"You stay here," I told him. "I'll finish up."

"If you mix up my cotton and polyester thread, so help me gods..."

I scoffed. "My own mate thinks so little of me. You think I can't distinguish between natural and artificial fibers? Please."

A slow grin spread over Taylor's face. "I knew I loved you for a reason."

I DIDN'T KNOW if it was a hormonal reaction stirred up by the rapidly growing egg, or if Taylor always threw himself this deeply into his hobby, but in the weeks following its delivery, he spent most of his time cozied up by the sewing machine. The rhythmic whirr of the machine became a familiar background noise. I'd often sit next to him and watch him work, awed by his focus and precision. He'd silently accept my offerings of tea and cookies, back rubs and sweet nothings in his ear.

"Finished," Taylor said as he sewed the last stitch into the millionth baby quilt he'd made. He drew it up for me to look at. It was a beautiful patchwork quilt with repeating pastel colors.

"This is wonderful, my love," I said. "Should I add it to the pile?"

Taylor nodded, already reaching into his fabric stash. I sighed. After putting the brand new quilt on top of the others, I returned and slipped my arms around the front of his chest so he couldn't instantly launch into a new project.

"Taylor," I said gently. "Don't you think it's time for a break? You've made at least twenty baby quilts in the past two weeks."

Taylor grumbled. "It's not enough. What if the baby needs more?"

"You're aware this castle is *full* of additional blankets, yes?"

"The baby needs to be warm."

"You're a five-hundred-pound tiger, I'm a fire-breathing dragon, and there's an entire pile of quilts on the bed. There's not a chance in hell this baby will ever be cold."

Taylor shuffled in his seat. "But—"

"These urges are your nesting instincts," I explained. "It's normal for omegas who carry eggs. And very adorable." I kissed him on the cheek. "But sometimes you need your alpha to pry you away from the sewing machine."

Taylor made a face like he wanted to argue, then sighed. "Fine. But I need to do *something.* I feel restless."

He got up and paced to illustrate his point. I regarded him closely. His belly was quite large. Aside from quilts, he'd also sewn some paternity outfits for himself so he didn't burst the buttons on his usual clothes. His unusual tension and urge to sew made me think he was closer to delivering than I first thought.

"Why don't you lie on the bed while I give you a massage?" I suggested.

"That's not *doing* something, that's having something *done* to me," Taylor grumbled.

I raised a brow, shooting him a stern, yet gentle look. "Taylor..."

The look was enough to push him over the edge of his indecision. He sighed, then slowly climbed into the king-sized bed. Moving around was difficult for him because of his size. My poor mate. The egg inside him must've been massive.

He couldn't lie on his stomach for obvious reasons, so he sat upright, propped up by a comfortable pillow. That allowed me to remove his shirt and access his back, which was often sore from carrying all that extra weight. A good, deep back massage would make him feel better, and hopefully distract him from the urge to sew.

I rubbed my thumbs into his shoulders, earning me a low groan from Taylor.

"Good?" I asked.

He grunted in affirmation, so I went on. I loosened up all the knots in his muscles, working my way down to his lumbar region. All the while, I appreciated his bare back, how strong and firm and masculine it was. He was my perfect match—I was incredibly lucky to have found him.

Overcome by emotion, I nuzzled his neck from behind, letting out a draconic purr.

"What?" Taylor asked, amused.

"Nothing. I just love you."

"I love you, too, lizard brain."

I pouted. "Hey, I'm being serious right now."

Taylor chuckled, then reached around to kiss me. "Sorry." He glanced down at his belly. "Actually, *you* should be the one who's sorry for putting this giant boulder of an egg inside me."

"But you look so sexy," I moped. "Besides, our baby's in there. You can't be mad at an egg."

"I'm not mad. I'm teasing." His hand grazed the back of my neck in a sultry, possessive gesture. "But next time, *you* try growing a watermelon in your body."

"Alas, fate did not bestow those parts on me. I would if I could, if only to spare you all this back pain."

He grinned. "I appreciate it."

After I worked all the tension from his back, Taylor let out a relieved groan. But despite it feeling good, there was still a small frown on his face.

"What's wrong, my love?" I asked.

He shook his head as he ran a hand over his lower belly. "Nothing, it's just this cramp..."

"Ah," I said, knowing full well what was about to happen. "I know it's sudden, but it might be time to lay that egg."

"What?" Taylor sputtered. "You're joking, right? I've barely been pregnant for more than a month!"

"Yes, but technically you've been gravid, not pregnant," I pointed out. "The egg has grown, but it still needs to be brooded outside of your body."

Taylor groaned, running a hand down his face. "Why'd I have to go and fall in love with a flying reptile?"

Behind the joke, I could tell Taylor was nervous. He liked to be in control, and laying a dragon egg was outside of his wheelhouse. It was times like this when I wished we had an omega in the family, or at least one in the castle. Why the hell did we all have to be born alphas?

I stroked Taylor's hair. "The most important thing is for you to stay comfortable. Use these quilts to nest. Hell, use anything in this room that strikes your fancy. I'm going to get you water and towels."

Taylor looked nervous. "You won't be gone long, will you?"

I kissed him on the forehead. "Just a minute. You won't even miss me."

"...Can you bring my pattern book?"

I ran over to his supply table, grabbed the book and gave it to him, then dashed out the door.

As soon as I stepped out of the bedroom, it hit me.

Taylor was laying our egg—right now.

The first dragon egg in our generation of Chromatimaeus dragons.

A sudden wave of panic hit me. Why did I have to be the first one to experience this? I didn't know what to do. I needed my brothers' help.

I ran around the castle like a basilisk with its head cut off. The unusual commotion drew attention from every bedroom door I passed.

Thystle's room was closest to mine. He poked his head out with a frown, his headphones halfway off his head. "Crimson, what's the rush? Your stomping is louder than Amy Lee's vocals."

"Egg!" I replied, already halfway down the hall.

That got his attention faster than his favorite band's tickets going on sale. I heard his rapid footsteps, but didn't stop to see where he went.

I ran straight to Jade's library. Out of everyone, I figured he'd have a clue about what to do. When I barged in, Jade stared at me in surprise. He didn't like to be bothered while he read, so I expected a quick snarl of derision, but when Jade saw my expression, he must've understood immediately. He leapt out of his seat, putting down his book.

"Is Taylor—?"

"Yes," I said breathlessly.

He gave a curt nod, then dashed to a different section of the library. "I'll meet you there," he called as he disappeared beyond stacks of books.

With that taken care of, I raced back to my bedroom. I hoped I hadn't kept Taylor waiting alone for too long.

On the way back, I almost crashed into the twins, who manifested out of thin air.

"Get out of the way!" I snarled.

"Hey, don't get mad at us," Saffron said mildly. "Look, we got towels and stuff!"

I blinked, calming down slightly. Aurum had a huge water bottle, while Saffron's arms were loaded up with towels.

"Sorry," I grumbled. "This egg is stressing me out."

"We can tell, grumpy pants," Aurum teased. "Come on, let's go help your eggy kitty."

"Do not call him that. By the way, how'd you know?" I asked as we booked it down the hall.

"Thystle told us. He said you looked so anxious your eyes were bulging out of your head."

I ignored that comment as we skidded towards my door. Thystle and Jade were already there. I assumed they were waiting for me. Cobalt stood silently a few feet away with a stoic expression. As the twins and I reached the door, I got a weird feeling in my chest.

"I'm here," I said. "Let me through."

Thystle and Jade both looked at me with uneasy expressions.

"The door's locked," Thystle said.

"What?" I snapped.

It wasn't locked when I left, and I knew Taylor wouldn't lock me out on purpose. The feeling that stirred in my chest got worse.

I rattled the door. It wouldn't open. It was locked from the inside.

"Taylor, are you there?" I called.

"Crimson," Thystle said quietly. "Just before I got here, I saw Viol go in. I asked him to open it, but he didn't listen."

My blood ran cold for a split second before it raged into a blazing fire in my veins. Viol was my brother. He wouldn't dare hurt my mate or my egg. But he was unpredictable. A wildcard.

My draconic instincts bubbled to the surface. A low, deep growl rumbled in my throat.

"Viol," I called.

My serious tone was enough to summon him. Judging by the creak of floorboards, he was right on the other side of the door.

"Crimson," he muttered in response, almost challenging me.

I struggled to keep my temper in check. If I shifted right now, I could break the door open—but that would cause Taylor unnecessary stress. I wanted his delivery to be as easy and comfortable as possible. I had to avoid a dragon fight at all costs.

But how could Taylor be comfortable with a stranger in the room? If Viol played games with me, he wouldn't like the outcome. My raging alpha instincts would fight tooth and claw to protect my mate and egg.

My dragon's voice overtook my human one, turning my sentence into a growled statement: "Open this door before you regret it."

The seconds that passed felt like an eternity. My brothers all held their breath in complete silence. Every moment that went by was a battle to contain my dragon.

And then, just before I lost my patience and shifted, the door clicked and swung open.

I rushed inside without sparing Viol a glance. I ran right to Taylor's side. To my massive relief, he was all cozied up beneath a pile of blankets. His pattern book lay at his side, untouched. Taylor's eyes were shut as he breathed hard, sweat rolling down his temples.

"Taylor," I said, kneeling beside him. "Are you okay?"

He peeked an eye open. "You lizard-brained liar. You were gone way longer than a minute."

I laughed in relief, kissing his forehead. If he had the strength to insult me, he was fine.

"I'm sorry, I was getting backup." I lowered my voice. "Did Viol hurt you?"

Taylor furrowed his brow. "What?"

I glared at my brother over my shoulder. He stood in the far corner of the room, expressionless and silent, just watching us.

"Him," I explained. "Did he do anything to you?"

Taylor blinked slowly. "Well, yeah." I was about to rip Viol's head off when Taylor added, "He brought me a hot water bottle."

"He... what?"

"He came in when you left and asked if I needed anything. To be honest, I was having an awful contraction, so I was in too much pain to be nervous of him. At that moment, I felt like I could've killed anybody who looked at me the wrong way," Taylor said, sounding embarrassed.

I laughed and nuzzled him. "That's my mate."

"But yeah. I snapped at him to get me a hot water bottle, and he did." Taylor blushed. He didn't like losing his temper, so that was a big deal to him. "And he gave me some extra blankets, too."

My white-hot rage towards Viol cooled, but not fully. I was still pissed at him for locking me out.

But that didn't matter right now. I had to tend to Taylor.

"My brothers are here to help," I said. "Is it okay if they come inside?"

"Sure, as long as they don't get in my swiping radius..."

I got up to give the others the green light, but when I turned around, I noticed Viol was gone. Putting my freak brother out of my mind, I invited the rest inside. Like Viol, Cobalt kept his distance, watching solemnly from afar. The twins did, too, though I suspected it was from fear of Taylor's wrath instead of respect. They were probably dying of curiosity to see an egg come into the world.

The ones closest to me were Jade and Thystle. I appreciated Jade's calming aura, and I suspected Taylor did, too. Meanwhile, Thystle gathered all the supplies and made them easy to access.

With a book propped up on his knee, Jade asked, "Have your contractions begun?"

Taylor nodded. "I've had a couple."

"How far apart?"

"Five minutes."

"Good, you're well along already." Jade smiled. "It shouldn't be long now. Dragon eggs have a tendency to come out sooner rather than later."

Thystle side-eyed the book on Jade's knee. "Yeah, but that's in dragon omegas. Does it work the same in other shifter species?"

"Taylor is a strong tiger. I'm sure he won't have any problems," Jade said calmly.

At that moment, a strong contraction ripped through my mate. He snarled, hissing through his teeth and clawing at the sheets. I put my hand on his shoulder. It was tense.

"Get these clothes off me," Taylor said. "It's coming."

A wave of panic coursed through me before my alpha instincts tamped it down. Now wasn't the time to freak out. Now was the time to protect and nurture my mate.

After quickly removing Taylor's clothes beneath the covers, I took his hand. He squeezed it with full force every time a contraction ripped through him, which came more and more frequently. I used a damp towel to wipe the sweat off his furrowed brow.

"*Fuck*, this thing is big," Taylor snarled. He opened his mouth to curse more when a wave of pain made him clench his teeth, doubling over with a roar.

Dammit, I wished there was more I could do. Omegas were so much braver than us. I doubted half the alphas I knew could tolerate this much pain without passing out.

"I'm here, Taylor," I reminded him.

I couldn't tell if he heard me over the sounds of his groans, but he squeezed my hand harder. It almost felt like he was crushing my bones.

Then Taylor's eyes snapped open as he stared at nothing. He stopped groaning, and his grip loosened on my hand. Except for the sound of his rapid breathing, the room was dead silent.

"What is it?" I asked.

Taylor blinked, then slowly sat upright, as if in a dream. He grasped the edge of the blanket and lifted it.

Just before I moved to look closer, I heard Aurum say, "Uh, is it just me, or is that blanket glowing?"

He was right. It *was* glowing.

Side by side, Taylor and I peered beneath the curtain of darkness... and saw a bright red glowing egg by his thighs.

I was speechless.

Our egg was here—and it was more beautiful than I could've ever imagined.

"What?" Saffron urged when neither of us spoke. "Can we see, too?"

I wanted to answer him that yes, he could, but the beauty of the egg literally took my breath away. Even in the darkness of the blanket cover, it shone in brilliant shades of red, like a perfectly oval faceted ruby. It almost didn't look real.

Taylor moved first. He sat up, pushing back the covers to reveal the egg.

My brothers gasped. They, too, were awestruck by our gorgeous egg.

"That's... what dragon eggs look like?" Thystle murmured.

"It's beautiful," Jade said as the red glow reflected off his lenses.

Taylor radiated relief, happiness and pride. He took the egg into his lap and curled around it, but his human arms weren't enough to satisfy his brooding instinct. With a growl, he shifted into tiger form to properly envelop his egg. He moved his big furry body until the egg was comfortably nestled in his side.

He sighed. "That's better."

Aurum snickered. "A tiger with an egg... that's new."

His twin elbowed him. "Congrats, you guys. Seriously."

The rest of my brothers joined in, ogling our unhatched baby and praising Taylor for the excellent job he did on laying a dragon egg.

"Let's give them space," Cobalt suggested. "Taylor. If you need anything at all, just ask."

Taylor nodded. He looked surprised to hear Cobalt speak since he was so quiet. "Thanks."

As my brothers piled reluctantly out of the room—their curiosity about the egg was tangible—I let out a sigh of relief to be alone with my mate again. I put my arm around his broad, powerful shoulders and nestled my face into his fur. It was warm and soft, better than any bed.

I realized I'd never been so close to his tiger form before. The other times I'd seen it were during challenges, when I wasn't allowed to go near him. I was glad the

Games were finally over so I could reap the rewards in peace.

"You did amazing, my love," I murmured into Taylor's fur. "I'm so proud of you."

The deep rumble of his appreciative purr made his entire body vibrate.

"Look at our egg," Taylor said.

I did. It got even more beautiful every time I looked at it. I reached out a hand to stroke its smooth surface. Watching the red glow disappear under my hand, then reappear when I removed it was magical.

"I still can't believe it was *in* me," Taylor murmured. "I'm surprised I didn't start glowing."

I chuckled. "Looks like we're both learning new things about dragon eggs."

Taylor flicked the tip of his tail curiously. "Crimson. What would you have done if you didn't choose me to win the Games? Would you have kept searching for a different mate?"

I gave him a serious look. "I didn't choose you, Taylor. Fate chose *us*. If you weren't here, I would still be alone. I'd go the rest of my life without a mate or an egg." I gave him a kiss on the tip of his tiger nose. "It's you, or nobody. That's all there is to it, my love."

His purr deepened, and his amber feline eyes glittered with affection. I could tell that was exactly how he felt, too.

Then his affection overwhelmed him, and he licked my face with his rough, scratchy tongue, causing both of us to burst into laughter.

TWENTY-THREE

Taylor
_____

MY TIGER SOUL had never felt so at ease.

I closed my eyes as I basked in the sun's rays. The white sand on the beach soaked up its warmth, each grain glittering like tiny diamonds under the bright blue sky. The sound of the ocean crashing gently on the shore was peaceful background noise.

It was interrupted once in a while by Crimson's younger brothers laughing and splashing each other in the water, but that was a peaceful sound, too.

"Do you think they'll drown each other, or is that too much to wish for?" Crimson teased.

I peeked an eye open and grinned at my mate. He lounged next to me on the beach towel. Our ruby egg, now a month old, sat nestled securely between us in its own personal towel. With the warmth of the sun, sand, and our body heat, I wasn't concerned about it being cold.

"I dunno, that's a big undertaking," I replied. "Can't lizards breathe underwater anyway?"

Crimson flicked a grain of sand at me while I chuckled.

Jade approached us, applying a new layer of sunscreen on his arms. "I know you're teasing, but most reptiles can't breathe underwater. So, yes, it's a possibility that Aurum and Saffron could die out there."

I snorted in amusement. "You don't sound very concerned."

He arched a brow. "Yes, well, a few of my books on *intimacy* have gone missing lately, and I'm inclined to believe they're the culprits..."

Crimson grinned. "Fratricide it is."

As if summoned, the twins leapt out of the ocean to join us. When both their heads were damp and their hair darkened by water, it was impossible to tell them apart.

"Calling them *intimacy books* is a really nice way of saying they were hardcore BDSM novels," Aurum teased. At least, I thought it was Aurum.

"Yeah, and they were really nasty, too," maybe-Saffron joined in, sneering playfully at Jade. "The kind with ropes and spanking and everything. Is that what you're into, Jade?"

Jade shot them a glare so icy that the twins dropped the smug act, turning sheepish.

"We'll, uh, go return those now..." they mumbled.

With that, the twins ran off.

As they flew off toward the castle, Thystle snorted. He sat fully shaded in his own personal umbrella. His sunglasses obscured his eyes, so I couldn't tell if he wore his usual eyeliner underneath. "I wouldn't be surprised if they keep those books. Y'know, for *research*. You might as well buy them their own copies."

Jade pinched the bridge of his nose and sighed darkly, like he was plotting the twins' demise. Then his frigid demeanor melted as he smiled at me. "How's the egg?" he asked.

I put a hand on its smooth shell, feeling a pulse of warmth.

"Decidedly cozy," I answered.

"May I?"

When I nodded, Jade kneeled down to run a hand over the egg with a thoughtful expression. "According to my notes on dragon biology, it's due to hatch any day now. You've done a wonderful job as first time parents, both of you."

Crimson and I shared a sheepish, appreciative smile.

Jade stood back up, casting a hopeful glance at the egg. "I'm glad the twins aren't around to hear me say so, but their idea ended up being useful after all. The Dragonfate Games brought you two together in a way I never expected."

"Me, neither," Crimson agreed, looking sweetly in my direction. "But if it means falling in love with Taylor, I'd go through all that nonsense a million times over."

Feeling too mushy for words, I leaned over to kiss him.

Then, Cobalt's deep voice came out of nowhere: "It pipped."

I would never not be startled when that man spoke. I didn't even know he was behind us until he said something, but I didn't understand what he meant. Looking behind me, I saw Cobalt—who looked funny wearing only swimming trunks—staring down at the egg.

I followed his intent gaze to the egg's surface... and saw the tiniest crack in the shell.

My heart skipped a beat.

"The egg," I whispered, sucking in a sharp breath. "Is it—?"

"Hatching," Crimson said with wide eyes.

"Wait, what?" Thystle cried. He tossed his headphones down on his beach towel, then bolted over to join the rest of us.

Time seemed to stand still as I stared, unblinking, at

the pip in the egg. It was happening. It was *really* happening —right now. Our baby was being born into the world.

I grabbed Crimson's hand instinctively. He put his arm around me, holding me for support.

My paternal omega instincts flared. "The baby can get out, right? What if it's a tiger and doesn't know how to exit an egg?" I demanded.

"It's all right," Jade said calmly. "The first crack in the shell is the hardest. It already pipped, which means it either has a baby dragon's egg tooth, or the tiger cub clawed its way out."

That relieved me slightly, but I didn't tear my eyes away from the egg. I'd be ready to help if necessary.

The ruby egg shifted, falling on its side. I gasped.

"That's good," Crimson told me with a gentle smile. "Look how hard our baby's fighting to get free. It's healthy and strong."

I growled. My instinct as a tiger to lick my newborn vigorously until it was clean and dry, but since his alpha father was a damned dragon, I had to wait until it was completely free of the shell.

The anticipation was too much to bear in human form. I shifted in one fluid motion into my tiger. My tail flicked impatiently and I paced around in the sand. I was this close to flexing my claws to unhook the pieces of shell when a *crack* resounded in the air.

Our newborn baby—a dragon—smashed a huge chunk of egg shell and thrust itself outside into the world.

No longer able to battle my instincts, I rushed over to my baby and licked it from snout to tail-tip, purring all the while. The newborn squeaked loudly in protest at being bathed. Good. My baby's lungs were strong.

Behind me, I heard Jade chuckle and comment to Crimson, "Your mate is incredible."

"I know," Crimson said proudly.

With my urge to lick satisfied, I shifted back to human form to pick up my baby. It was my first time getting a good look at them, and they were just as beautiful as the egg they grew in. Their scales were a reddish-amber, like a mix of Crimson's scales and my tiger's orange pelt, but the most surprising part was the stark black stripes, like a tiger.

Crimson laughed, joy emanating from his voice. "Would you look at that? A striped dragon!"

"That's a first," Jade commented.

Thystle's lined eyes shone wet with tears. He sniffled, wiping his face. "I can't believe it... We've got a baby in the family."

A large, warm hand touched my shoulder. It was Cobalt. For the first time since I'd met him, he smiled.

A pair of rowdy voices in the sky grew louder. Aurum and Saffron shifted midair, touching down in the sand and running over.

"We missed it!" Aurum cried. "All because of those stupid books!"

Jade was too enthralled by the baby's presence to chide his brother about calling books stupid. He gestured for the twins to come closer.

The golden twins went wide-eyed at the sight of the baby. Saffron, apparently the more openly emotional of the two, cried tears of happiness.

"Hang on," Crimson said. "If you two were in the castle, how did you know the baby hatched?"

"Viol told us," Aurum said.

Crimson frowned. "What the—? He wasn't even here."

Aurum shrugged. "Maybe he was lurking in the bushes or something. Anyway, who cares? Look at the widdle stripey baby. Yes, that's you! Cute little guy..." He poked a finger towards the baby's mouth—and promptly got bitten by a row of tiny dragon teeth. "Ow!"

Crimson laughed. "That's my kid, all right."

I pulled the sassy baby dragon into my lap. They instantly calmed down, nuzzling against me and eliciting a group "aww" from Crimson's brothers.

"Call me ignorant about dragons, but how do I tell if my newborn is a boy or a girl?" I asked.

Jade chuckled. "When baby dragons hatch, they tend to stay in that form for a while. You might not know until the first shift."

"Yeah, it's not like a mammal where you can just lift the tail and know," Aurum chimed in.

I smirked up at Crimson. "So, what you're telling me is..."

Crimson sighed dramatically. "Yes, we *are* essentially overgrown, fire-breathing lizards."

I grinned, relishing in the joy of finally winning this debate. "Thank you for admitting it."

"Have you guys picked a name?" Saffron asked.

Our baby yawned, then settled back into my lap. I smiled at Crimson.

"It's a little on the nose, but we picked a classic dragon name," I said. "Ruby."

Nobody seemed to mind that it wasn't the most original name in the world. Crimson's brothers were too busy welcoming Ruby into the family, cooing and gushing over them.

As I watched, I felt overwhelmed with love. After being left behind by my biological family, I didn't know if I'd ever feel welcomed in a familial setting again. But Crimson and his brothers filled that loss, replacing it with something good and whole. As we all gathered on the beach, happy for the newborn dragon and hopeful for the future, I felt truly at home on Chromatimaeus Island.

My mate leaned over to kiss me. He shared my wavelength, as always.

"I would say the hard part's over, but with a newborn dragon, it's just beginning," Crimson teased.

I shrugged. "Small, striped, lots of teeth and claws... I'd say a baby dragon is pretty similar to a tiger cub."

He chuckled. "So you're up for the challenge if we want a second?"

I kissed him again, but this time, I gently bit his lower lip. "Don't push your luck, lizard."

Cobalt's deep voice summoned everyone's attention. "We should celebrate. Barbeque tonight on the beach."

"Dude," Aurum said, looking excitedly at me. "You haven't lived until you've tasted Cobalt's lambchops."

My tiger soul licked its lips. "That's a great idea. But are you sure you want to go through all that work, Cobalt?"

The corner of his mouth turned up. "You and Ruby are family. And I would do anything for my family."

Aurum groaned. "That's nice and all, but we don't have time to gush! If we're throwing a BBQ, we have to prepare! Where'd we put the sheep-sized tongs again?"

Crimson and I shared a grin as his brothers raced around. This was turning out to be an exciting day, indeed.

TWENTY-FOUR

Epilogue: Crimson

THE SCENT of grilled meat and veggies filled the crisp evening air, and smoke danced upward towards the blue-black sky. Above the gentle sound of the ocean waves on the shore was my family's voices, laughing and arguing and swooning over the newest addition.

Cobalt manned the helm—AKA, the barbeque. He was dressed in leather sandals and a simple grilling apron. Jade helped him cook by double-checking the internal temperatures of the meats. Eating raw meat wasn't a problem for dragons—or tigers, honestly—but Jade wanted to be safe. Thystle argued with the twins over whether or not goat and sheep meat tasted the same. Viol was missing, but after our last mysterious encounter, I wasn't convinced that he wasn't lurking nearby on the fringe of our activities.

Meanwhile, I sat with Taylor on a double-seater beach chair with Ruby tucked snugly between us. Baby dragons spent a lot of time asleep, which was a nice break from the chaos to come as they grew older—and bitier.

Taylor sighed wistfully as he leaned his head on my shoulder. "This is nice."

I smiled and touched my head to his. It *was* nice. It was too peaceful to even make a snarky remark about how Thystle had Aurum in a headlock, or how Jade chided Cobalt for slightly burning the meat. Everything just felt right.

Since Ruby spent so long sleeping and Taylor couldn't sit still for two seconds, he pulled out a small sewing kit from his beach bag. Apparently since finding out about the barbecue, he'd whipped something up, but I hadn't seen the final product yet.

"What is that?" I asked.

He put the final stitch into the fabric, then set the needles away. "There. Done."

As he held it up to show me, I laughed. "It's perfect." I glanced over to the grill. "Hey, Cobalt! Come here for a second."

Cobalt reluctantly handed control of the grill to Jade, then approached us. "Is something wrong?"

"Nothing's wrong. Taylor has something for you," I explained.

Cobalt's brows raised. "For me? Why?"

Taylor got up from the chair, then pulled out the pile of fabric from behind his back. Cobalt took it with a look of confusion.

"Open it," Taylor urged.

Cobalt let the fabric fall to its full length. It was a Cobalt-sized BBQ apron, complete with a "Kiss the Cook" inscription, and a blue dragon applique.

Cobalt was a quiet man, but I never thought I'd see him speechless from emotion like this. A full minute passed before he finally moved. Instead of speaking, he pulled Taylor into a bear hug. Or, dragon hug, I suppose.

Taylor laughed in relief, patting him on the back. "I'm glad you like it."

Cobalt nodded. When he pulled away, I thought I saw a tear in his eye. He put on the apron immediately, and it fit him like a glove. I didn't expect anything less from my mate. I shot a beaming, proud smile at him. The pride reflected back in Taylor's eyes.

There was something else shining in his gaze, too —love.

Family love for my brothers.

Parental love for Ruby.

And deep, fated, soul-bound romantic love for me.

Holding Ruby in my arms, I stood up to give Taylor a kiss. With the sounds of the lively beach surrounding us, we kissed under the evening stars. Love swelled around us, enveloping us like the warmest quilt in the world.

"Hey, you two!" Aurum called, waving us over. His plate was already full to bursting. "Come eat before we take it all!"

Cobalt swatted Aurum's hand with his tongs. "Leave some for Taylor and Ruby," he growled.

Just in time. Ruby yawned, blearily blinking as they woke up from their nap. I could already see the hungry gleam in my baby's eyes.

I laughed. "Uh oh."

"What's wrong?" Taylor asked.

"If there's one thing to know about baby dragons, it's that they *always* wake up hangry."

Taylor grinned. "Then let's grab food before Ruby eats Aurum's whole hand this time."

THE END

Don't miss Thystle's story in the next book: Alpha Dragon's Eagle!

Want to see Ruby's first shift? Get the bonus scene by signing up to my newsletter!

Printed in Great Britain
by Amazon